RAVE REVIEWS FOR T. M. WRIGHT!

"T. M. Wright is a rare and blazing talent."
—Stephen King

"T. M. Wright has a unique imagination."
—Dean Koontz

"Like Stephen King at his best, Wright can hold us shivering on the edge between laughter and fear."
—*Newsday*

"T. M. Wright is a master of the subtle fright that catches you by surprise and never quite lets you go."
—Whitley Strieber

"Wright convincingly proves that he understands, as few do, how to give a scare without spilling blood all over the page."
—*Publishers Weekly*

MORE PRAISE FOR T. M. WRIGHT!

"T. M. Wright is more than a master of quiet horror—he is a one-man definition of the term."
—Ramsey Campbell

"I have been an unabashed fan of T. M. Wright's since reading his first novel."
—Charles L. Grant

"T. M. Wright's nose for horror is as acute as Stephen King's."
—*Fear*

"Without doubt, Wright is one of the most interesting horror writers out there."
—*At World's End*

"A producer of work of the highest caliber. While many other authors may be sweating over their next supernatural extravaganza, Wright seems to deliver these delicious pockets almost effortlessly. His narrative is so sharp it makes a lot of writers seem clumsy by comparison."
—*Horrorworld.com*

THE FIRST KILL

I want to talk about my first kill.

I need to talk about my first kill. It stirs something sweet inside me, it stimulates me; I do it all over again, I satisfy that first, wonderful agonizing need and lust all over again, I break that boy's skin and the life beneath rises up and spills over my tongue and into my throat like butter.

I could never taste the blood, though I've always so wanted to.

It was a young boy whose name was George. He lived two miles from the house on Phillips Road and he was coming home late from school and I swept over him with my arms wide and I remember he turned around and began to laugh at me because he thought it was a joke.

Then I tore him up.

And oh I am going to do the very same thing to this man one of these evenings when I'm through with him.

Other *Leisure* books by T. M. Wright
SLEEPEASY

T. M. WRIGHT

THE LAST VAMPIRE

LEISURE BOOKS NEW YORK CITY

A LEISURE BOOK®

November 2001

Published by

Dorchester Publishing Co., Inc.
276 Fifth Avenue
New York, NY 10001

ISBN 0-8439-4939-2

The name "Leisure Books" and the stylized "L" with design are trademarks of Dorchester Publishing Co., Inc.

Printed in the United States of America.

Visit us on the web at www.dorchesterpub.com.

For my muse, in absentia

THE LAST VAMPIRE

Prologue

———

2047

Our beliefs mold us, define us, and dictate the course of our existence. If we believe that we are good and kind and generous, then that is how we'll act, and the world will love us. If we believe that we're controlled by unseen and malevolent forces bent on the destruction of all that is noble, benevolent, and altruistic in our culture, then we shall find ourselves under the control of these forces—whether they're real or not— and the world will despise us.

About my friend, Elmo Land, vampire

I met him after a party on September 9, 2047. It was a dreary party—as all of us at the house expected. My cousin Stacey threw the party and invited 1000 people whom she culled from local Net searches. Most of whom she invited said they would not attend, and most for the same reason—"Requires social interaction." Some pointed out that parties were "grandstanding of the worst sort"; one said that parties would bring about the "destruction of the Net, as we know it, which has been our lifeline after the Obscenities of the Last Generation." I agreed with that assessment. Who needed actual physical contact, after all, unless it was necessary? Hadn't it been shown that physical contact, outside the Net—touching hands, elbows, shoulders, feeling the breath of others on our cheeks and backs, seeing emotion in their eyes (unfiltered by the Net's pleasant bioelectronics), the resentment inevitably generated by the *need* to touch coupled with the need for *space* and *distance*—results in despair, degeneration, hurt, and mayhem? So why a party? I asked my cousin.

She merely smiled and said, "Because I think it's time."

The house here, where the party took place, has triple doors in all the hallways (quadruple doors in the longer hallways), as well as stout bolts everywhere. No unfiltered viewing of other inhabitants of the house takes place unless it's requested or required.

Twenty-three arrived at the house for the party. This made a total of fifty-one souls, including the twenty-eight who lived at the house. It was an unwieldy number, I told Stacey, and it would result in a lot of unfiltered contact; "Which," my email told her, "will provoke a caustic steam of resentment and disharmony."

More than an hour later (she's never punctual), she wrote back, "Put a sock in it, Harpo," which was not unlike her. She's a throwback. She listens to Beatles music ("Come Together" echoes through the house at odd hours) and reads the poetry of Gary Snyder and Galway Kinnell ("It wouldn't interest you," she wrote once. "It's not synthetic or electronic or soulless, and it *sings!*"). She calls me Harpo (after Harpo Marx) because, she says, he too avoided actual verbal interaction, preferring, again according to Stacey, "the bells and whistles of *his* generation."

My room is small, square and contains no uncovered windows. I have my Book in it, of course, and it rests on a small honey pine desk. The chair I sit in when I'm using the Book is sturdy, also made of pine, and I've put a soft pillow on it for comfort. I have chosen to use a keyboard rather than voice activation for my emails because I find the touch of the keyboard oddly exhilarating. Several others in the house have told me they experience the same exhilaration, and that it makes them uncomfortable—they believe it says something about an innate or instinctive need for the tactile; I choose not to think about it.

Stacey's party began at 6:00 P.M. and there were visitors standing at the door at precisely that moment. She attempted to embrace these visitors (oddly, most accepted her embraces) before ushering them into the house's great room, where she had asked all of us to congregate. I told her of course that I wasn't about to congregate and neither were most of the others who inhabited the house, except for Steve and Lorraine, who live together in two rooms and have grown used to congregation, and Rudy, who pretends to be an artist and, he tells us, needs congregation. But, to please Stacey, I went to the great room, anyway.

I believe that at the party's peak, there were eighteen souls congregated in the great room and thirty-three in various small rooms within the bowels of the house; some of this number had gone off to individual rooms as couples, and some had gone off alone, though all carried their Books with them. During the party's brief life, much emailing was accomplished.

The party ended ninety minutes after the first souls arrived. It was an abrupt ending. Stacey emailed everyone that the party was over—she was, in fact, somewhat shrewish about it; "This has been a mistake," she wrote. "I have made a terrible mistake. You must leave now." And everyone did.

I pulled my curtains aside and watched the last pair

of visitors leave, Stacey waving goodbye to them from the driveway. It was early evening, though some crisp sunlight lingered. I could see the tall, black rectangular silhouettes of the city and of the closer trees (just then beginning to lose their leaves), and Venus twinkling gaily near the red horizon. I couldn't see much of the visitors who were leaving, only the suggestion of coats and skirts moving languidly in the semidark. When they were gone, I saw Elmo Land for the first time. He was simply a face, then, barely visible as a creamy oval. But, over a period of moments, he became a face and light-colored jacket, then hands, too, and what could have been jeans—though this was only a guess, from my vantage point. It took half a minute, I think, for him to completely establish himself in the area where I had seen him begin to take shape.

Stacey lingered in an area close to him, though it was clear to me that she didn't see him. She could see me looking out my window, I assumed, because she raised her hand in a jittery wave, then made quickly for the house.

Elmo Land did not move. I assumed that he, too, was looking up at me, for I saw the creamy oval of his face, the darker ovals of his eyes, the smaller oval of his mouth. After a minute, his mouth moved a little, and I heard, "May we talk?" I jumped back from the window and let out a kind of *Urp!* because the voice had sounded as if it were in the very room with me. When I stepped back to the window, Elmo Land was gone.

My nights are as restful as anyone's. Fifteen minutes asleep, according to my Book, then fifteen or twenty minutes of wakefulness; this process lasts the night, then the Book tells me it's time for the day to begin.

I was in the middle of this process—during hours of near total darkness—when I became aware that I was not alone in my room. It wasn't the first time I'd experienced this feeling. I have experienced it now and again for most of my life, and I've always felt the presence of the Book itself accounts for it, because the Book is another intelligence that shares our rooms with us—an intelligence that does not sleep and that minds our lives. I have assigned a personality to this nighttime presence, a personality that is part predator and part caretaker. It seems to fit the Book well. When I've sensed a nighttime presence in the past, I have also always sensed that personality, so whatever fear I might experience at first always dissipates quite quickly. It did not dissipate quickly this night because the personality I sensed was not the personality of the Book. It was a human personality.

I did not sleep the rest of the night.

That human personality returned the following night. I sat up and said, "Are you the one who spoke to me?" though I could see nothing in the room—not the gray rectangle of my windows, not the darker gray rectangles of my bureau, my desk, my chair.

A man's strained but oddly pleasant tenor voice—

the same voice I had heard the previous night—said, "I need to talk. May we talk?"

I said nothing for a moment. A tall gray lump established itself in a corner of my room and I fixed my gaze on it, though I saw nothing definitive. I said, at last, "Yes."

"Good," said the voice. It sounded elated. "Good. We'll talk." Then the gray lump was gone.

It returned later that morning, when darkness was still upon the house. It became more definitive; I saw the suggestion of hair and eyes, hands, a mouth. "I'm Elmo Land and I need to talk with you," the lump said.

I said, "Yes, I wish you would. Do you come from the Book?"

"No," said Elmo Land. "I don't believe that I do, at any rate."

"Are you an apparition?" I said.

Elmo Land said, "Yes." A second later, he added, "I believe that I am an apparition. It's one of those things."

"One of those things?" I said.

"Yes, one of those things we pass through, one of those moments," said Elmo Land. "One moment we're a living person, we have the needs of a living person, the next moment we're an obscenity, then, moments later, we're an apparition. I believe that at this moment in my existence, I'm an apparition." He paused, seemed to cock his head. "Do I frighten you?"

"Yes," I said.

"I understand," he said, "and I ask your forgiveness. I believe that I can . . . disappear and still hold some semblance of a conversation with you. Would that be better?"

I thought about this and answered, "I don't think so. I'm not sure. It would be disconcerting."

"Yes, I understand," he said. "And for me, too. Disconcerting."

"Are you one of many apparitions?" I asked.

"I'm one," Elmo Land answered. "I don't know about others. I believe there are probably many others. Perhaps billions. Sometimes I think that I hear them. But who can see them? Not I. The place where I exist is a . . . maze of hallways and corridors . . ." He stopped.

"Yes?" I coaxed.

"And who sees anything but walls?" he said.

I said nothing. His head seemed to move a bit, as if he were glancing about the dark room. Then he added, "And an occasional glimpse of gray sky, but I know that it's a gray sky I saw as a child, or when I was becoming an adult. I recognize it. I see birds in it and they're flying somewhere. North, I think, and so I know it's springtime, or at least I believe that it is—a dead springtime when I last saw that particular gray sky and those particular birds." A quick sound, like a brief chuckle, came from him. "So I know that it's a memory I'm seeing, that has made itself real to me." He paused, continued, "It's a blessing. The walls here hold memories, if we know how to see them, if we choose to see them."

"We?" I said.

"Whoever. I know there are others. I hear them. They cry out names, or they simply cry out. I hear them. They sound as distant as stars. But who knows? I think they're a wall's depth away, the length of a large hand from my hand, perhaps." Another brief chuckling noise came from him. "I sound as melancholy as a goodbye note, I think. Forgive me, again. Circumstances. You become dead and then you become . . . an . . . obscenity. An obscenity. But it passes, and you become . . . this—it makes you crazy, I think."

I said, "And you're here because . . ."

Another brief chuckling noise. "Because I've always wanted to write, to tell stories, hell, *my* story, too. Ever since I was . . . what?—Just undead." A pause. "You don't understand that. How can you? It's simple, but who understands it? 'Just undead'—it sounds remarkable, unbelievable. It is."

"Yes," I said.

"And there you are, with that . . . thing . . . what do you call it?—Your Book. I want to use it, but I can't. Not in the way that you use it. An apparition using a keyboard? It's unheard of, I think. It's unbelievable. Remarkable. Can't touch, can't smell, can't see . . ."

"You don't see me?"

"How can I? It's too dark. Turn on a light."

I didn't want to turn on a light. I didn't want to see *him*.

"You don't know that I'm joking?" he said. "How can that be?"

"You're joking?"

"I'm saying that I want to use your Book but I can't because I can't *touch* or *smell* or *see* or *hear*. . . ."

"You can't hear me? How can we be having a conversation if you can't hear me?"

"Good Lord, I hear *you*, not your voice. I see *you*, not your face."

I said nothing.

He said, "Do you understand?"

I answered, "But how can *I* see and hear *you*?"

"In the same way that I see and hear you, my friend. What other way is there? We live in different . . . houses."

"I don't understand," I said.

"Who cares?" he said. "You may never understand, not in the life you're living now. . . ." I believe that he sighed. "Listen, I just want to use your Book. It won't take long. A few minutes. Perhaps longer. Perhaps an hour, three hours. A couple of days. What does it matter? You'll have my story when I'm done. And you'll love my story. It sings."

"But you just told me that you can't *feel* anything . . . how do you expect to use the keyboard?"

"I don't need to *use* the keyboard. I don't need to *speak* to your Book. Just as I don't need to see your face, or hear your voice. . . ."

"But the Book isn't alive. . . ." I said.

"We'll find out, won't we?" he said.

Barely a day later, all that follows had become a part of my Book. I didn't see Elmo Land again. I suppose he was done with me. And those words, "We'll find out, won't we?" were the last words I ever heard from him.

You might ask what I make of his narrative. I note that it's divided into two sections—one written in third person, the other—much longer, more poetic, I think, and more despairing—in first person. My assumption is that the third-person narrative is somehow less reliable as history than the first-person narrative, though I have no concrete reason for thinking this. It also occurs to me that the entire "Cowboy Narrative" may be Elmo's attempt at fiction, while all that follows—starting with "My name is Elmo Land"—may be a more accurate and autobiographical account. I note that the "Cowboys" do not appear in the much longer, first-person narrative, although the English professor does, as do "Hiram and Betty," "Georgie," and "the singing woman." It also may be that Elmo—who certainly is not a temporal being—may be recollecting events and emotions in a very tangled and confused way, which would account for the disconnectedness of the third-person narrative and the occasional dreaminess of the longer, first-person narrative. All of this is, of course, mindless speculation, because it occurs to me, as I type, that I am trying to psychoanalyze an amazing creature who, for only part of his existence, was a human being.

I have also tried to reconcile dates and historical events in both the third- and first-person narrative, though with little success. I do know that there was an apocalyptic confrontation between what was then known as "The Super Powers" some fifty years ago, from which our present Book and email culture arose. I do know that, in the late 1920s, there was a financial collapse called "The Great Depression," about which Elmo speaks briefly in his third-person "Cowboy" narrative. The other events of that narrative are, I believe, basically unreliable—and, I'll say again, possibly an attempt at pure fiction—because Elmo couldn't have known all that he claims to have known about the "Cowboys" without actually having accompanied them on their various escapades. This may simply be a matter of artistic license; or, if Elmo was at one time what his narratives claim him to have been—a vampire—then the comings and goings of others of his kind may have simply been a part of their culture and collective intelligence. In other words, all in that culture knew what all others were doing because the spiritual bond they shared was so terribly and demonically strong.

I've shared both narratives with several of the others in the house and their response has been mixed. Stacey asked if it was I who wrote them, and although I assured her I had not—that I actually *could not* have written them—I think that she remains doubtful. Steve and Lorraine wanted to know who I thought the "woman singing" might be, and I hadn't much of an idea, which I told them. Steve asked, "And what does he mean when he says, over and over again, 'You are what you eat'?" Again I had to confess ignorance.

Elmo's "Cowboy Narrative," as he titled it, may also be a kind of wish fulfillment. It is often light and amusing, although some of the events it recalls are horrific, and this may be a way for Elmo to absolve himself of the awful crimes he confesses in both narratives. This idea melds easily with the tone of his brief appearances here, in my room.

I miss him. That is to say, I miss the world or worlds that he gave me a microscopic but tantalizing glimpse of—the worlds of the afterlife. I wish him well in his journeys. I hope those journeys bring him back to this house, however briefly, and to this room, and into my Book.

The Cowboy Narrative

Elmo had been on the midnight rodeo circuit for a couple of months and had been tossed about by bulls and broncos, and by the occasional cowboy, too; he had even served a short stint as a rodeo clown—when a man got thrown from whatever animal he'd been attempting to ride, Elmo bravely put himself between the man and the animal. He supposed that the pain from multiple kicks and falls would have been excruciating had he been able to feel it, and he was thankful that his acting abilities—good to superior, he thought— had survived with him after his death. Otherwise, he supposed, even the cowboys would have found him out in no time.

He had struck up a close friendship with a short, stringy man named Llewellyn who chewed tobacco and spit a lot, and who was partial to homey philosophizing about a man's place among "horses, dirt, and cow shit." Llewellyn wore bright red chaps, a bright red shirt, and a bright red vest when he rode, and Elmo thought the combination of colors—Llewellyn's hair was shoulder length and prematurely gray—made him look like a number-2 pencil with arms. More than a few times, Elmo had been at the point of the "great confession" with Llewellyn. He thought Llewellyn would understand and sympathize, that he wouldn't judge, laugh, or disbelieve, as others had. But Elmo never made the great confession to Llewellyn because Llewellyn died. This happened on the evening that Elmo had set aside to make the great confession, a very hot evening in July.

He'd primed Llewellyn for the great confession this way:

"Llewellyn, after you ride, I need to talk with you. It's important."

"Sure," said Llewellyn, spit out some chewing tobacco and sauntered off to his Brahma bull—bright red chaps, vest, and shirt catching the hot light of the arc lamps nicely. Minutes later, the Brahma bull kicked Llewellyn's head nearly clean off.

Elmo remembered standing over him and crying. He found this surprising. Why cry? he wondered. What was the difference? Llewellyn was just one more of the very bloody dead. There were so many of the dead, and most of them had little to say.

Elmo remembered that Llewellyn's blood was nearly the color of Llewellyn's shirt, his chaps, and his vest, and that it pooled around his head like a fan. Elmo remembered bending to it, putting a finger in it. He remembered Llewellyn's gray matter splayed out in the yellow dirt in the shape of the letter *W*. Elmo thought this was prophetic, that someone with the initial *W* might one day figure prominently in his existence. He remembered wondering if *W* would be the first initial or the last initial. Perhaps it would be both. *W. W.* William Weeds, perhaps. He'd known a William Weeds, but that man was dead now and not speaking much.

"Jees, look at him," Elmo remembered another cowboy saying. "Jees, that cow really kicked the shit out of him. Ain't got enough brains left in his head even to spit!"

Elmo remembered nodding.

"Ain't seen nothin' like it since my brother's boy got caught in a hay baler," the same cowboy prattled on. "Gawd, *that* was a sight!"

Elmo merely nodded again.

"Jesus Christ, Elmo," the cowboy said, "I do believe yer cryin'." He slapped Elmo on the back. "Well, I think that's nice. Old Llewellyn here probably ain't got no one to cry over him 'cept you, so I think that's real nice." Elmo was surprised by the cowboy's words. Cowboys weren't supposed to weep, after all, or to give much latitude to men who did weep.

"He was my friend," Elmo said.

"Then you got a right to weep," said the cowboy. "Ain't at'all manly, of course. Not somethin' men do. But that's assuming a lot, ain't it?"

Elmo turned to look at the cowboy, saw him grinning hugely, big, bright white teeth reflecting the arc lamps. The cowboy repeated, "Ain't it, Elmo? Ain't it assumin' a lot?"

Elmo said again, "He was my friend."

The cowboy slapped him hard on the back once more. "And still *is* your friend!" His grin became conspiratorial. "He's just a *dead* friend, now. And they're the best kind!"

This annoyed Elmo. The man had huge brass balls to make jokes at a time like this, when poor Llewellyn's gray matter lay all over the yellow dirt. "I told you," Elmo reiterated, "he was my *friend*. And if you can't treat him with respect . . ."

"We got all kinds'a respect for poor dead Llewellyn," the cowboy broke in. "I mean, look around you."

Elmo glanced about. All the other cowboys—fifteen of them—had come to within a couple of yards of Llewellyn and had formed a half circle around him. And all of their pasty-white faces were cast downward, their hands were clasped, and their eyes were closed.

"He was one of the finest humans we ever knew," said the cowboy.

*

Three years later, a professor of English at New York University said to Elmo, "Let me tell you about vampires." He and Elmo were in a diner on Second Avenue and it was 10:00 in the evening. The diner was all but empty, except for Elmo, the professor of English, and a tall bag lady at the counter who was leaning over to sip her hot chocolate without lifting it from the countertop. Elmo and the professor had ordered Cokes, but they had so far gone untouched. The professor went on, "Vampires are egocentric."

"I know that," said Elmo.

"No, no, I don't think you do. I think you're agreeing with me without realizing the depth of egocentricity that I'm talking about. I'm talking about a depth of egocentricity that is . . . life threatening. . . ."

"Vampires aren't alive," Elmo said, lifted his glass of Coke, touched it to his lips, and put it down again.

"Oh, of course they are," the professor of English said with a dismissive wave of his hand. "They're ambulatory, they're sentient, they react to stimuli . . . of course they're alive. Hell, they can even *reproduce*, and isn't that a certain test of life?"

Elmo looked suspiciously at the professor of English, who added, "They're simply not alive in the same way that they once were. They're not alive in the same way as"—he glanced about, nodded at the bag lady—"as she is."

"Which is to their credit," Elmo said, and again

brought his glass of Coke to his lips without drinking from it.

"Why do you do that?" asked the professor, meaning why did Elmo pretend to drink from the glass of Coke.

"I have to," Elmo said. "It's comforting."

"Nostalgic, you mean?"

"Yes."

Elmo knew the names of some of the cowboys arrayed around Llewellyn's broken body. They were good cowboy names—Slim, Dusty, Rowdy, Clint, Gil, Blackie, Swiftie, Mack, and Tom. Two of the cowboys, in fact, were named Tom. One called himself Tom Mix. He was short and rotund, but his skin sagged, as if only air lay beneath it. These cowboys all wore ten-gallon hats, brightly colored chaps, and expensive cowboy boots that they polished to a high shine after every midnight performance. They were good cowboys, too. They rode well, they roped well, they seemed to accept pain as if it were merely part of the performance. And they were all consummate showmen. But Elmo had trusted none of them, though he wasn't sure why. Perhaps, he thought, it was because he sensed a kind of dishonesty in them, as if they shared a secret among themselves that they were not about to share with him. Llewellyn was different, though. Llewellyn made his life and his thoughts an open book. He was not as good a cowboy as the rest, but he was more open, more genuine, more . . . human. And, oddly, this appealed to Elmo. Plus, Llewellyn let Elmo talk about himself at length, which was something the other cowboys wouldn't tolerate; and Elmo loved to talk about himself.

The professor of English took a great swallow of his Coke while Elmo looked on in awe. "How can you do that?" he asked.

The professor put the half-empty glass of Coke down hard enough that the bag lady glanced quickly at him, and he answered loudly, "Hell, Elmo, we can do anything we damn well please. You didn't know that? And why wouldn't we be able to do anything we please? What limitations do we have? We aren't answerable to God, or to the devil. We're answerable only to our appetites."

"I'm not as pathetic as all that," Elmo said.

"And who said we were pathetic? We're . . . supermen. We are! Hell, we can fly and bullets can't touch us."

"I can't fly," Elmo protested.

"Well, of course you can't actually *fly*, Elmo. Of course you can't actually flap your arms and go off into the wild blue. But you can *will* yourself to go any fucking place you want."

"To the moon? To Mars?"

"I don't know. I've never tried. But now that you mention it, shit, I *will* try it. Not that there would be anything interesting on the moon, or on Mars. There certainly wouldn't be anything to satiate . . ."

"Who said we have no limitations?"

This seemed to stump the professor. His broad brow furrowed; he glanced down at his half-empty glass, then up at Elmo, then out the window.

Elmo repeated, "Who said it? Who said we have no limitations?"

The professor answered, with a touch of surliness, "I did. *I* said it."

"Oh," Elmo said with an approximation of a sigh. "*You* said it."

The rotund cowboy who called himself Tom Mix stepped up to Llewellyn's broken body, bright blue ten-gallon hat in hand, and said, "Hey, Llewellyn. I see you got kicked in the head, there. I 'magine it hurt some. Had a sister got kicked by a eighteen-hand plow horse and she done nearly lost all her brains, too. Oh, what a sight, Llewellyn!" And he stepped back, head lowered.

Another cowboy stepped forward, his green ten-gallon hat in his hands. This cowboy's name was Mack McGordy, and he was very tall, very thin, and very white. He spoke in hugely sepulchral tones: "Llewellyn, you poor bastard," he said. "you know you got to watch out for bulls. They'll kill ya just as soon as piss on ya. And I guess you got killed real bad by this particular bull." He paused, then added with a smile, "And that ain't no bull!" which, Elmo noticed, made all of the other cowboys smile.

Mack McGordy stepped back and another cowboy—he called himself Blackie Kincaid—stepped forward, his black ten-gallon hat in hand. Blackie was big and muscular, so muscular, in fact, that his black shirt strained at his buttons and his black pants strained at his thighs. He was also fidgety. He looked nervously right and left, at no one in particular, and moved his hat around in his hands as he said, in a voice that was oddly high-pitched, almost feminine, "You done had the big fall"—he paused—"so now you got no brains at all." The cowboys smiled quickly. "But it weren't a fall, it were a maul"—a pause—"that done you in, and that's a sin." All the cowboys smiled. "You was good, as good as wood"—the cowboys frowned—"as good's you should"—the cowboys frowned again—"and if you ship your brains to Helen"—his third wife—"she'll know for sure they're from Llewellyn"—the cowboys smiled—"and if you believe"—a pause—"then roll up your sleeve, 'cuz there's work to be done"—a pause—"but not in the heat of the midday sun!" He paused dramatically, then repeated, "But not in the heat of the midday sun!" He broke out in a great toothy smile. All the cowboys broke out in great toothy smiles. Mack McGordy stepped forward and slapped Blackie hard on the back. "That's the best yet," he said. "The best yet!"

"Yeah," gushed Blackie, "I think so."

And another cowboy said, "Hey, we gotta *eat!*"

The professor of English picked up his half-empty glass of Coke and studied it a good long while. Then he put it down and looked questioningly at Elmo. "You think we're *bad?* Is that what you think?"

Elmo said nothing. The question was stupid. Who in the hell thought in terms of "good" and "bad" anymore?

The professor went on, gesticulating wildly, head bobbing and shaking at the same time—as if he were suddenly going to come apart—"Who's *bad?* Who's bad? Is the lion *bad* because it devours the fucking zebra? Is the volcano *bad* because it buries ten thousand people in molten goddamned lava? Is . . ."

"I get your point," Elmo cut in.

"Don't interrupt me," snapped the professor, and gave Elmo an imperious wave of his hand. "You keep interrupting me! I got things to say, and my God they're important! So you just listen, and if you can't listen, well, maybe you should get outta here and go for a walk."

"Good Christ!" Elmo whispered.

"Good Christ *nothing!*" spat the professor. "He was no better than any of us. No better than you or I or the fucking Dalton gang. He was programmed to do whatever the hell he did—heal the sick, raise the damn dead, walk on water, talk in fucking parables—just as we're programmed to do whatever the hell we do—drink blood, sleep in coffins, all that shit!"

"I don't sleep in a coffin," Elmo protested. "I sleep in a cellar. It's on East Ninety-eighth Street."

"Cellars, coffins," cried the professor, "what's the fucking difference? It's a box. It's in the dark. Same fucking thing. What I'm *trying* to say, Elmo, if you would stop interrupting, is that we are all *programmed* to do whatever the fuck we do—from the goddamned lion to the fucking volcano to fucking Jesus H. Christ, on up to us. And you know who the fuck does the fucking programming?" He paused, then nodded with great enthusiasm as he went on, "You know *who? God!* It's *God!*" He closed his eyes quickly, opened them wide, shouted, "God! That lousy bastard! Programs us and punishes us, programs us and punishes us! Stupid, I know. Shows that's he's no fucking Rhodes Scholar . . ."

A high-pitched feminine voice cut in, "Hold up there, you're talkin' 'bout my dear Lord and personal savior, Mister!"

The professor looked toward the source of the voice.

The bag lady was glaring at him, hot chocolate all over her mouth.

"Fuck your personal savior!" the professor said.

The bag lady got off her stool.

The professor shouted, "And fuck you, too, and fuck this goddamned restaurant . . ."

The restaurant's owner—a beefy man in a white T-shirt and white pants—appeared from the kitchen and hollered, "Why'nchtall get the fuck outta here! Hell, you sit in my place for hours and hours and all you ever order is Coke and hot chocolate!"

"Yeah, let's go," Elmo said.

"Fuck them all!" cried the professor, and stood suddenly.

After the cowboys ambled off and the people from the local volunteer ambulance service arrived, Elmo said to one of them—a chunky woman with long dark curly hair and a smile Elmo didn't understand, considering the circumstances—"He was my friend. Llewellyn was my good friend."

The chunky woman was lifting Llewellyn's legs at the time, and a thin man with a wispy mustache was lifting Llewellyn by the arms. What remained of Llewellyn's head was lolling backward, so his long gray hair hung in the yellow dirt. "Good to have friends," said the woman, and another cup of Llewellyn's gray matter fell from his head and hit the yellow dirt with a muted *whump!*

"Jesus, Mary, and Joseph," said the thin man with the wispy mustache.

"You got that right," said the chunky woman.

"It's his damned brains. Don't you know that?" Elmo said.

The chunky woman's odd smile faltered. "Yeah, I know it's his brains. I seen brains before. We all seen brains before."

"Jesus, Mary, and Joseph," the thin man said again, as he and the woman carried Llewellyn off.

Elmo called after them, "Hey, where you taking him?"

"To the morgue, where do you think we're taking him?" the chunky woman called back.

"And where's that?" Elmo called. "Where's the morgue?"

But they didn't answer him, and moments later, they'd loaded Llewellyn into the ambulance and were gone.

The professor of English walked with his hands thrust hard into the pockets of his baggy gray pants and his head down, as if he were in thought. He mumbled something that Elmo couldn't hear.

"Did you say something?" Elmo asked.

"I said that I gotta kill something. If I don't kill something, I'm going to go crazy!"

Elmo thought the professor was crazy already, though he said nothing.

"We're all of us crazy," said the professor. "All of us who do what we have to do. We're crazy."

"You're talking about everyone," Elmo said.

"Shit on you. I'm talking about us." He still had his hands thrust hard into his pockets, but he was looking at Elmo as he spoke. "I'm talking about *us*. God's cast-offs." His eyes were round and dark. "We're not men. We're not much of anything at all but *need*." They were on East Forty-second Street. Most of the storefronts were dark and there were few pedestrians. Occasionally, a yellow cab passed by. Elmo could hear steady soft footsteps far behind him and the professor.

"Do you hear that?" he said.

"Of course I do. I'm dead, not deaf."

Elmo smiled.

"You like my sense of humor?" asked the professor.

"I do. I always have. It sings. It's electric."

" 'I sing the body electric . . .' " said Elmo.

"Yeah, don't we all," the professor said, and made a snorting sound that Elmo had come to know as a chuckle. "Whitman was great. A faggot who devoured little boys. I love it. Such poetry."

"It's that woman," Elmo said.

"I know it's that woman. Fuck her. She's got some plan for us. Shit. She's our soup du jour."

"You think so?"

The professor glanced around, in the direction of the footsteps, then at Elmo. "Yeah, I think so."

"What plan?" Elmo said.

"To take our money. She thinks she's going to hit us over the head and take our money. Big plan. Shit on her."

"How do you know that's her plan?"

"Idiot! I know it's her plan because I can *hear* what she's thinking! What's the matter—*you* can't?"

"No. How do you do it?"

"Oh, for the love of God. Elmo, there's no *way* to do it, it's something you simply *do*."

"I can do it sometimes," Elmo said. "I can hear what people are thinking sometimes."

"Good for you," the professor sniffed, and stopped walking.

Elmo stopped walking.

The professor said, "We'll wait for her."

"Why?"

"Stop asking stupid questions."

A cop car cruised by and slowed, but kept going.

"Lousy cops," said the professor. "Like to take your freedom away."

"Do you really think she wants to rob us?" Elmo asked.

Again the professor said, "Stop asking stupid questions."

The cop car cruised by again, backwards, slowed, stopped. A spotlight shot out at Elmo and the professor, and a male voice demanded, "You two up to something?"

"Yeah," the professor snarled back, "we're walking here. There a law against it?"

"You got some ID? It's pretty early in the morning to be out walkin'."

"ID!" snapped the professor. "Yeah, I got ID. You want ID, Mr. Flatfoot? Shit, then—I'm Jack the Ripper!" He made the snorting sound that Elmo had come to know as a chuckle. "And my friend here is fucking *Santa* Claus!"

A door opened on the cop cruiser.

Elmo said, "Jees, what did you do that for?"

"Ask me if I give a flying fuck!" said the professor.

"And why are you so angry?" Elmo said.

"Angst," said the professor.

Llewellyn was laid out naked at the coroner's office, two rooms in a converted barn not far from the town of Albion, not far from the village of Hootie-Hoo, a stone's throw from the hamlet of Lakeville, a hundred miles north of Atlanta.

Elmo thought that Llewellyn looked very ill—naked and dead. His skin bore the bluish tint of early dawn and his long gray hair was matted with blood. One eye was gone and the other stared at the ceiling. Elmo leaned over Llewellyn and looked into this staring eye. He thought he might see a bull's hoof there—which would have been the last thing Llewellyn saw. He also hoped he might see his own reflection. But he saw only the tin ceiling overhead. He sighed. He'd grown used to rejection by mirrors—but this was his late friend's *eye!*

The coroner came into the room. He was a stout man of six feet, and he wore a well-coifed beard. He was wiping his hands on a towel when he saw Elmo.

"And who the hell are you?" he said.

Elmo did not turn to look at him. Elmo was still trying to find his reflection in his dead friend's eye. "I'm this man's friend," Elmo said.

"Be that as it may, you have no right being here."

"I have every right being here. I'm this man's friend."

"You're an intruder and you'll have to leave."

Elmo ignored him. He thought he was beginning to see the faint echo of his own reflection in Llewellyn's dead eye.

The coroner came forward a few steps. "Something's not right about you. I can sense it."

Elmo said nothing. He thought that his reflection was growing clearer, and he was elated.

"You'll have to give me your name," the coroner demanded. He was still wiping his hands with a towel. "If you don't, I'll call the police."

"Shut up!" Elmo said.

The coroner inhaled sharply.

"You're annoying me," Elmo added, still looking into Llewellyn's dead eye.

"Oh my God," breathed the coroner, as if in shock, and turned sharply to his right, toward a phone on the wall.

"Don't do that," Elmo said.

"The hell you say," the coroner shot back, got to the phone, lifted the receiver from the hook, and began dialing.

He noticed a strong and noxious odor before dying. It was oddly similar to the odor he had lived with every day during his two decades as the county coroner. But this was the first time he had noticed that odor on the living.

The cop facing the professor was a bear of a man whose blue uniform fit very tightly, and when he spoke, his sibilants were punctuated by spittle. "I know your kind, mister," he said, and pushed a huge finger into the professor's chest.

"I doubt that," the professor said calmly.

"I know your kind real good," the cop said. "You like to start trouble. You think us cops are stupid."

The professor grinned at the cop. "I think your grammar is as atrocious as your breath."

The cop grinned back and poked his finger harder into the professor's chest. "Yeah, well, look who's talking. You got the breath of a dead man, and I ain't lyin'."

The cop's partner appeared from the other side of the cruiser and stood stiffly near Elmo, who was standing near the professor. The second cop said, "This don't feel right, Hardy."

"Feels right to me," Hardy declared. "Feels real right. Feels right as rain, and I ain't lyin'."

"You already said that," the professor said.

Elmo said to the second cop, "You'd better put a leash on your friend. Otherwise, you'll both regret it."

The second cop said, "That a fuckin' threat?"

Elmo said, "Yes, it is. It is without a doubt a fucking threat."

The second cop quickly unholstered his .38, pointed it stiffly at Elmo, hand shaking, and barked, "You get your hands in the air." He thought a moment, then amended, his voice shaking, "Better yet, get on the ground! Now!"

Elmo looked silently at him for a moment, then said, "You really don't want to be doing this."

"Get ON the ground, NOW!" the cop shouted, and waved his .38 to indicate the pavement.

The professor said, "You'd better do as the officer requests, Elmo."

Elmo gave the professor a questioning look.

The professor said, smiling, "It'll be fun—getting on the ground, being handcuffed, going to jail, being booked and fingerprinted . . . the whole . . . shtick. It'll be a learning experience." Hardy still had his finger poked into the professor's chest. The professor added,

"Or we could simply emasculate them here and now . . ."

"You shut your filthy mouth," Hardy barked, and poked his finger very hard into the professor's chest.

"You know," said the professor, "make them eat each other's balls. . . ."

Hardy pulled out his .38 and in the space of two heartbeats pointed it at the professor's head and fired. But Hardy was a lousy shot. The bullet missed the professor's head by inches—even though Hardy held his .38 at point-blank range—and hit Hardy's partner in the neck, severing his Adam's apple and exiting through the top of his spinal cord. Then the bullet hit the cruiser's right rear window, where it left a small, neat hole.

"Oh, shit, God," Hardy said, and watched his partner, whose arms were straight at his sides, crumple to his knees, hesitate for a moment—as if in grim indecision—and fall face forward to the pavement with a quick, soft, wet *whump!*

"Christ almighty," Elmo said, though more in annoyance than fear.

"Gimme that damn thing," ordered the professor, and snatched the .38 from Hardy's hand.

Hardy looked blankly at him for a moment, then at his fallen partner, then at the professor again, who was looking questioningly at the .38; "Very efficient little thing, isn't it?" the professor said, grinned crookedly, and shot Hardy in the face.

T. M. Wright

A Vampire Christmas

The midnight rodeo crew always had a very large, well-decorated and beautifully lit Christmas tree. Their December circuit took them through an area where many species of pine thrived, so they went, as a group, into the countryside very early in the morning—between 2:00 and 4:00 A.M.—hatches in hand, in the week before Christmas, found the largest tree that time, and the impending sunrise, would allow them to find, and had at it until the thing fell. Sometimes their happy activity aroused the curiosity of land owners, hunters, or campers, and the poet of the group, Blackie Kincaid, was dispatched to charm the curious and the suspicious:

He told them,

> " 'Tis a bleak thing to cut a tree.
> The earth doth tell us, Let it be.
> And oh we listen, and oh we weep
> While the harmless tree doth sleep
> And dreams of leaves and summer skies
> Forest creatures, a happy sunrise.
> But we are on a higher calling
> That says this tree just must be falling.
> For if it don't, then we can't show
> Repentance to He who makes it grow.

For we are killers, one and all,
And that is why this tree must fall."

This satisfied practically no one, of course, though Blackie always hoped it would. So, after hearing the poem, the curious or the suspicious were almost always summarily dispatched and thrown into a deep hole hastily dug. One man—large, potbellied, and apparently very happy, because he smiled constantly—thumped Blackie on the back when the poem was done and declared, "By Gawd, that is truly the worst thing I have *ever* heard, but I'll tell ya, you do say it nice," which did not please Blackie one bit, because he thought his poetry was timeless—just as he was—so he took not one, but two great chunks out of the smiling man's neck. Then, using the same ax he'd been using to help chop down the group's Christmas tree, he chopped the man into pieces small enough to be fed to forest rats.

Getting the tree back to their rodeo site was always very time-consuming. None of the fifteen in the group had a valid driver's license, though some still carried licenses that had been valid when they were alive. The problem lay in the fact that each of the cowboys loved to drive; not only was it nostalgic for them, but their new persona gave them an affinity for machines that was magical—as if they and the machine were truly one. So they took turns driving. It was barely five miles back to the rodeo site, but each of the fifteen cowboys had a turn at driving their old Ford truck, freshly cut tree hanging out the back. Which meant, of course, that they had to stop quite often, but this was okay. It was clear to them that the spirit of sharing was an important part of the Christmas season.

And while they involved themselves in the time-consuming but happy process of finding and felling a tree, then bringing it back to the rodeo site, each cowboy was decked out in brightly colored, freshly washed chaps, vest, and ten-gallon hat, because this was, of course, his costume, the face he presented to the world of the living.

They bought new lights for their tree every year, at Woolworth's or JCPenney. As a group—and always after sunset—they drove their old Ford truck to whichever store was closest to the rodeo site and, moving single file through the narrow aisles (which were always crammed with Christmas items), they spent many loud minutes discussing which lights would be best for the particular tree they'd chopped down, and for that particular Christmas.

"I've always hated these big colored lights," Tom Mix

said every year, holding up a box for everyone to see. "I've always thought that they were too big and too bright. Especially for this skinny tree we got."

"And what's wrong with big and bright?" Rowdy always shot back.

"Well, it hurts my eyes," Tom Mix told him.

"You gotta wear sunglasses," said Gil Hawthorne. "And besides, that tree ain't skinny. It's got a good girth."

"You know I can't see if I'm wearin' sunglasses," Tom Mix said.

"Besides," said Clint, "this is a Depression Christmas, so we gotta try and make people feel good, don't we? People gotta feel good, 'specially if they're gonna come and see us. And if they don't come and see us, then where the hell are *we*, huh?"

"People always feel good about the rodeo," said Dusty Rhodes. "They come for that, not for the Christmas tree. They come to see us ride the bulls and such, not to see no tree full'a big colored lights."

Tom Mix put down the box of colored lights. "What'sa matter, you don't like Christmas?"

"I like Christmas fine, you know that," Dusty Rhodes answered.

"No, he doesn't," said Blackie Kincaid. "Just the other day, I heard him say, 'I wish that Christmas would go away.' "

The same words, the same give-and-take, every

Christmas since the cowboys had been performing their Midnight Rodeo, which, in 1930, had been nearly a decade.

Cowboy History

In life, Tom Mix, then known as Thomas M. Sizemore, worked for a very large advertising firm in Chicago. The firm had multiple accounts, but their largest account was with the then-largest tobacco manufacturer, Chestnut Tobacco, based in Georgia. Chestnut wanted Tom Sizemore's ad agency to show the public that smoking was actually *good* for health, and for the spirit, and that it was especially good for men who really wanted to *be* men.

One day, Tom Sizemore told the head of the advertising agency that he had to take a couple of days off to take care of his horses.

"You ride horses?" asked the agency head, in awe.

"Yes, I do. I've ridden them all my life."

"Doesn't that take a lot of stamina?" asked the agency head, who was very large and usually very out of breath.

"It does, yes," said Tom Sizemore.

"And yet you smoke. Does that have any effect on your stamina—I know it does on mine." He smiled quickly; he didn't like revealing his ill-health, and liked even less revealing that it was probably related to his smoking habit, which was as huge as he was. After all, he had to project a positive attitude toward all things having to do with tobacco if the people under him were going to believe in the product they were advertising.

"I do smoke, yes," said Tom Sizemore. "Several packs a day. And I have to say that it has never had an effect on my stamina. . . ."

"You'd say, in fact," interrupted the agency head, "that it has had a generally *positive* effect on your stamina, wouldn't you?"

Tom Sizemore began to answer in the negative but thought twice about it, realizing what the agency head wanted to hear. Tom said, "I'd have to say that smoking has . . . made me feel like a man . . . just as riding horses does. . . ."

"There you have it," declared the agency head. "By God, there you have it. You've said it all, right in those short sentences. Smoking makes you feel as much like a man as riding horses does. Tom, I think we've got our campaign."

After some discussion, Tom agreed to go to a ranch in the Midwest—along with several of the agency's photographers—where he would show the world, through photographs, that smoking was necessary to "make a man feel like a man."

"But why just one man?" the agency head wondered. "Why not several? Why not a dozen or more?"

"But where are we going to find them?" Tom asked.

"Why, right here. At the company," answered the agency head.

So, on May 3, Tom and a mix of ad writers, accountants, layout men, artists, and photographers boarded a train in Chicago for Randall's Western Ranch, near Grant City, Utah. It was the last time that most of them, as living men, would see Chicago.

"That whole thing was really unnecessary," Elmo said.

"Nothing's unnecessary," said the professor.

"Now *that's* damned stupid," Elmo said.

"Whatever happens happens because it was meant to happen, otherwise it wouldn't," said the professor.

Elmo looked confusedly at him. They were walking side by side on Second Avenue, near a line of small shops—delis and grocery stores, a printer's shop, a laundry, all closed—and Elmo could hear the bag lady's footsteps not far behind them. Several long blocks off, Officer Hardy and his young partner lay dead.

The professor said, "Hey, we got other stuff."

"I didn't much like killing those cops," Elmo said.

"Yeah, so?" said the professor.

"It was stupid," Elmo said.

"A stupid and necessary act in a stupid city on a stupid evening in a stupid year," said the professor.

The footsteps behind them grew suddenly quicker and louder. Elmo said, "She's running."

"I feel very good," said the professor, "I feel energized—like I just got a shot of adrenaline. Don't you feel it, too?"

Inside a laundry on the opposite side of the street, Elmo saw the whisper of movement.

Behind them, the sound of footsteps grew rapidly louder, closer, more urgent.

"Hey," Elmo said, "something's happening on this street."

The professor looked at him and smiled—though Elmo had no idea why—then looked away. "The movements of the living and the agonized," he said.

"Your riddles," Elmo said.

"Death's a riddle," said the professor. "Death's a fucking riddle. First life was a fucking riddle, now death's a riddle." His gaze was lowered and he was smiling, clearly pleased with himself.

"Have you always spoken in riddles?" Elmo asked.

"I think that I have, yes," answered the professor, and gave Elmo a quick, broad, dark smile.

Behind them, the running footsteps were very close.

On the opposite side of the street, a male figure emerged from the darkness behind the laundry window and fixed its gaze on Elmo and the professor.

A high-pitched female voice screamed, "Die, devils! Die!"

"It's the bag la . . ." Elmo said, and stopped, because he saw that the professor had turned about, that the bag lady was standing in front of him, that something had been stuck into the professor's chest, and that he was clutching it and looked surprised, awed, fearful.

It has always been a mystery why that train slipped the tracks. It wasn't speeding, and the tracks were straight—they had, in fact, been laid only three years earlier, so they were in nearly perfect shape. A later examination of the cars themselves revealed no mechanical problems that would have caused the train to derail. It was as if, one writer put it, "the hand of God, or Satan, came down and lifted that train from the tracks." Of the 200 people on board, 123 were killed instantly in an inferno caused by ripped gasoline storage cars that had—foolishly—been put in the middle of the line of passenger cars. Fourteen others died en route to hospitals, another twelve died at the hospital, and fifteen—the men from the ad agency, including Tom Sizemore—were officially listed as missing. This was particularly puzzling to investigators. In the entire history of train wrecks, only a small handful of people, in total, had ever been listed as missing, and this usually happened when a train plummeted into a river or a lake and the bodies were washed away. The train that the men from the ad agency were on derailed on dry land, near the hamlet of Mohochomo, in southern Utah. Some speculated that the raging fire had obliterated their bodies completely, though others asked why *these* men in particular? And besides, investigators noted, the car in which they'd been riding had been barely touched by the fire.

About Mohochomo

It is a hamlet composed of very large houses and very old people. No children live in Mohochomo, so there are no schools, no playgrounds, and no candy stores. It also boasts no gas stations and no grocery stores because none of its inhabitants drive and, it is said, all provide food from their own gardens. Mohochomo's youngest inhabitant, of a total of sixty-three, is reported to be not quite seventy and its oldest just past one hundred. According to census records, poorly kept because the inhabitants of Mohochomo rarely answer their doors and have never filled out census forms, no families live in Mohochomo. Its sixty-three citizens inhabit forty-seven large houses. At one point in its long history, a *Stop* sign was installed at the juncture of Main and North Main—Mohochomo's only streets—but this sign disappeared within a week and was never reinstalled.

Not much traffic moves through Mohochomo. Getting to the hamlet requires leaving the main paved highway—route 43A—and getting onto several passable dirt roads. Nonetheless, people do drive through Mohochomo because, from a distance, it looks picturesque—large, Victorian homes nestled in a peaceful valley.

One person who drove through it, not long after the train wreck that killed so many, told of seeing young male faces peering vacantly out the hamlet's numerous windows. . . .

The Dreams of a Vampire

are dreams the earth has, dreams that leaves have, and clouds. But they are dreams that are as human as tears. And they bind the way that age binds. When they're finished, they leave us with fragments of so many lives, done and undone. And we put these fragments together the way an insect might put together a symphony—some may find sense in such a construction, most cannot. But, ultimately, *sense* resides in all things.

. . . look, I have apologies for little Georgie, whose head went *Sploosh!* into a rock,

and to Hiram and to Betty, who were doing only what their God told them to do . . .

and to God Himself, who should have known better than to create such creatures as we . . .

. . . I remember Christmas, and I remember fishing at a thousand lakes, and learning to love, and I remember the taste of bad whiskey . . .

*

What better way for the cowboys to survive—to entertain, to eat, to sleep, to entertain, to eat, sleep, and so on, and so on, and so on. For decades, I think. *Oh, a Midnight Rodeo,* cried the great unwashed. And they came by the dozens, then by the hundreds. They saw pale men in brightly colored chaps and vests ride and rope like experts, ride and rope so well, in fact, it was almost supernatural, they said. And they saw the cowboys fall sometimes, too, as if the cowboys had momentarily lost their earthly balance. Falling this way and that, off horses, bulls, fences, on solid ground. Not often enough to arouse anyone's suspicions; no one ever wondered, *Why do they fall?* Because cowboys always fall. Sometimes gracefully, and sometimes to their deaths. But these pale cowboys—most of them, anyway—always got up and rode again, and again, and again. For decades, I think. Until circumstance—bad luck, accident, God himself—stepped in and brought them down forever and ever. . . .

Amen . . .

Amen . . .

Look, I have apologies for everyone. The ego persists, the ego eats and survives. Blame it on that. On ego and appetite. I have . . .

Amen . . .

Apologies to Georgie whose head fell apart . . . and

to Hiram and Betty . . . and all the innocents . . . and to Christmas . . . to the singing woman . . .

Amen . . .

To no one . . . to myself . . . I remember myself . . . bawling my little blue eyes out waiting for a breast . . . eating a breast . . . enjoying a breast . . . breast blood . . . breast milk and breast blood . . . what a stew . . .

But the cowboys survived long enough. There's a monument to them somewhere. It shows two pale cowboys in bright vests and chaps and ten-gallon hats on two horses that are side by side, and they're riding well, so well, in fact, that some called it supernatural. . . .

Look, who needs to apologize? We do what we do and we can do nothing else except what God designs us to do, and so it's his fault that we do what we do. . . .

Look, Georgie needed killing,

Look, Hiram and Betty needed killing,

Look, brain matter everywhere, like snow, everywhere, like gray water, like snow, brain matter sloshing about . . .

So, I am.

I persist, even now. Persist. Persist. Resist. Cannot go away. Leave nothing, take nothing, break hearts and bones, hearts and bones . . .

We dream the way that rocks dream. And trees. Light. Deserts. Lakes.

We do not send Christmas cards.

1

March 18, Tuesday

For some time now I've had an idea for a short film, a kind of comedy vignette. I planned once, in fact, to actually produce it. I thought somebody on *Saturday Night Live* might like it, or maybe David Letterman, or it might even have ended up as an HBO short. It involves a couple of anonymous Vampire Hunters who, after years of searching, finally track down their prey in a predictably dreary castle somewhere in Transylvania, steal into the chamber where his body lies, place the dogwood stake to his heart, breathe "Die, Evil One!" (or somesuch) and drive the stake in hard. At that moment, of course, the vampire wakes, looks incredulously at his chest, smiles, and breaks into song: "Peg oh my heart," he sings, "I love you, Peg oh my heart!"

I never produced that comedy vignette, of course. Not for lack of funding, just lack of initiative. And, of course, HBO, *Saturday Night Live*, and David Letterman have all gone the way of the dinosaur.

*

I wear a blue and gray striped polo shirt, yellow, loose-fitting cotton slacks, Nike tennis shoes, and white athletic socks with a red stripe around the top. These are all brand new and very comfortable. The cotton pants "breathe" well, the polo shirt stretches the way *I* stretch, the Nikes have a good spring to them, and the socks provide an extra "cushion" of support, which is helpful because my feet have been flat since the day I was born.

That was in 1907. So if I had lived I'd be not quite one hundred years old now.

I miss having birthdays. Everyone does, I think. I see them lying around spread-eagled, or hugging themselves, as if for warmth, and piled one on top of the other and they whisper to me that they never ever thought it was going to be like this, that they had expected something a bit more final, or a bit more ethereal. But they wait inside themselves, instead, and watch their bodies come apart, and they feel the awful pain that they were so certain death was going to bring an end to: but they were wrong, of course.

I want to tell them, *Hey, I've had that same pain for eighty years, now. The only difference is, I've got to walk around with it.* But I don't tell them that. Maybe because they've got enough to worry about.

I am Elmo Land, born 1907 in Hanford, Kentucky, to Myrna and Elmo Land Sr, who died in a house fire in 1929. They're buried side by side in a quaint country cemetery near Jackson, Mississippi, which would have been their wish, I think—to be buried side by side, near Jackson—if they'd been given the chance at a last wish or two. They were good and generous people who loved each other without qualification and who gave what they could of themselves to their only child. It was to their credit, I think, that the only thing they had in abundance to give me was time.

A woman named Regina Watson moved into a big house down the road from us in Hanford early in August, 1927, and when I first saw her she was washing her front windows with a whitish rag that she dipped often into a rusty milk bucket filled with water. She had a long row of six tall, narrow windows to wash on the first floor of her house, and she washed them with a vengeance—it was a still, hot and quiet morning and I heard the shrill squeak of that rag against glass long before I could see the house.

My father sent me there. "Go introduce yourself, boy," he told me, and leaned forward in his cane-back rocker (the only piece of furniture that survived the fire in 1929) and whispered, "Jus' don't let your ma know!"

I watched Regina Watson from behind a waist-high, gray picket fence for several minutes. Her back was to me; I supposed she could see my reflection in the window she was washing because she was in shadow, on the porch, and I was in sunlight. But when at last I said "Hi" she froze. I said "Hi" again, and she turned very gracefully around and looked at me, the wash-rag dripping onto her plain white dress.

"Who are you?" she said. She appeared to be in her

late twenties, and what I supposed was a naturally dark complexion looked to have paled. She wore her black hair in a tight bun at the back of her head; her face was a delicate oval, her eyes large, her mouth small, her nose straight. She appealed to me at once, on several levels, and I found myself grinning foolishly at her and hoping, at the same time, that she didn't notice.

I nodded to my right. I said, "I live down the road there. My name's Elmo Land."

She had a look of panic about her, like a deer at night when caught in the beam of a spotlamp; and as I see her now, with the eye of memory, eighty years later, I think that in many ways she was much like a small bird trying desperately to survive in a world populated by bigger birds.

But she did survive.

She was exceedingly good at it.

"What do you want?" she said.

"Just to introduce myself," I answered. I was not quite twenty then, and shy, especially around women, and especially around intimidating women, as she was, though I doubt she realized it.

"You have introduced yourself," she said, and turned back to her windows. She had not said it unkindly, she had merely been dismissing me.

So I went obediently back home, and on the way there I started thinking about her, and about how she'd affected me.

*

I told my father, "She scares me, Pa. She scares me a lot." It made him laugh; he laughed often—a loud and usually infectious laugh. This time, I realized that he was laughing because he'd put something over on me. "'Course she does, boy," he said. "All good-looking women is scary, I'd say." He paused, then added, "And she's crazy, too, of course!" He laughed again. When he was done, he went on, "Didn't I tell you she was crazy?" which made him laugh once more.

"No," I whispered. I was upset with him because he'd tricked me. "You never told me nothin' like that."

He was halfway into his five-day growth of beard, then. He let it grow five days, sometimes six, then cut it off, usually with a straight razor much in need of sharpening, which made him curse repeatedly while he was doing it. (He called himself a farmer; he grew potatoes on a couple acres of muck behind the house, and occasionally corn and tomatoes on bad acreage west of the house. His harvests were usually poor, some years there was no harvest at all, but we never lacked for food or clothing, because he was very good at making whiskey.)

He swiped at his two- or three-day growth of beard—believing, I think, that there was something in it left over from a meal, though there wasn't—and said, "I really should have, boy. I guess I should have. But she is. She'll bite ya." He pointed at his neck to indicate his jugular. "Here." He grinned. He liked to grin—he knew that he looked friendly and approachable when he grinned because he'd had an expensive set of dentures installed several years earlier and he kept them well polished. "She thinks she's a vampire, Elmo."

And I said, "What's a vampire?"

He said, "Someone who bites you in the neck, I guess," laughed yet again and continued, as he laughed, his voice rising in pitch with each quick breath, and his dentures whistling at the same time, "Someone . . . who bites you . . . in . . . the neck, Elmo. Someone who's crazy and bites you in the neck." Which, on reflection, eighty years later, does not seem like a very kind thing to say, but is nevertheless pretty close to being accurate.

But my father was wrong. Regina Watson was not a vampire. She kept one. She called it Luke.

She kept Luke in a small room in the west wing of her house, and I saw him there a week after my first encounter with her.

Wednesday

Pain today in the thighs, deep in the bone, and I sense something alive here, too, something close enough, I think, to shout at.

Thursday

Luke was naked and filthy in a corner of the room Regina Watson had put him in and he was wide-eyed as if in terror, his forearms tight to his ears, his hands clasped behind his head, and his knees up, under his chin. His mouth was open a little, and a constant, middle-pitched humming sound, like the voice of a boy just past puberty, came from him.

I had a friend with me when I first saw Luke. His name was Lemuel and he was my age, my size—tall, thin—but he was clumsy and dull-witted.

Lemuel said, "He ain't got no clothes on at all, Elmo," and grinned up at me from his crouching position at the window. "He's teched some I think."

It was a warm, bright afternoon and there were dozens of fat honeybees buzzing all around us in the grass. One of them stung Lemuel in the right temple and he whooped with pain and fell to the soft dirt just under the window, his hand pressed hard to his temple. He stopped whooping after a few seconds and whimpered, "Oh shit Jesus Gawd, Elmo, that hurts!"

I told him, smiling, that I was sure it did. Then I saw that Luke had mashed his face into the window so his nose was flat and his nostrils flared, and Lemuel saw him too, and he skittered away on all fours, like a crab, shrieking "Jesus Gawd he is, he is!"

Luke vanished.

Friday

This village is called "Mumford", and the people who lived here and died here are like most of those that died. They are confused and angry that they were forced to die. *Not so much for myself,* some of them say, *as for the children.* And, *It's the pain we don't like,* which seems to be a common theme. But when I try to talk to them about *my* pain they don't listen, and I begin to believe that this is a one-way communication, that they can talk to me, but I can't talk to them. I don't know. Maybe Death has made them all bull-headed and desperate.

And what about heaven? some of them say. I shrug. What do I know about heaven?

One person is alive here. He's hungry, as I am, and he's frightened, young, reasonably healthy. It will be good to talk with him a little when he screws some courage up, because it's clear that he doesn't know yet what to think of me; I can hear him say to himself, "Good Lord, who in the hell is that?" Which tickles me.

Saturday

I attempted masturbation again. I got the old urge, like the urge to smoke, but it worked as badly as smoking does, because my lungs haven't worked for eighty years, either.

He masturbates, I can feel him masturbating, and I can see what he sees in his fantasies, but it doesn't do a thing for me because he has his ideas of what's stimulating, and I have mine. At least I used to.

I think often at times like these that it would have been much, much better for my well-being if I had not died a virgin.

As little Luke was.

Sunday

Around me, some of the people lying dead whispered that they wanted to go to church today. Old habits die hard, they said, and because I know quite well about old habits, I took one of them—a man in his sixties dressed in blue denim farmer clothes, and in an advanced state of decomposition so his pain was very bad indeed—into a pretty, white clapboard building called the Mumford Free Methodist Church, and I propped him up in one of the rear pews. I had no idea what else to do for him. I wasn't about to play the part of a minister—though once, as a child, I gave a kind of "practice sermon" at the Baptist Church my parents attended.

Several years after my death and transformation, I snuck into a theatre in Baltimore to get out of the sunlight and the noise and I put myself far back in the balcony so I could watch Bela Lugosi pretending earnestly to be what I *was*. I wondered, *Why does he speak that way?* and I answered myself, *Because he's Hungarian*, which didn't satisfy me. *It's an affectation*, I thought, having recently learned what "affectations" were in a night class in English Literature at the University of North Carolina.

And there, in the Mumford Free Methodist Church, I thought of calling up that affectation, and using it on the poor fool I'd propped up in the pew.

I wanted to ask him, too, why he hadn't done anything to stop the war that killed him. But I didn't. I had no way of knowing if he did nothing. The chances were excellent, I knew, that he was simply an innocent victim of circumstance. As most of us are.

I sat with him awhile; I experienced his pain, on

top of my own, and when that became too much, I left him alone.

He's still propped up there, in one of the pews, and I expect that he'll stay there for quite some time.

2

___

April 2, Wednesday

Little Luke, Regina Watson's boy, looked just like a plump, over-stuffed, white nylon doll whose mouth has been made from two folds of its own nylon skin stitched tightly together, whose eyes have been fashioned from tiny bright blue buttons, and whose nose seems very much an afterthought because half of it is missing and the other half is ragged and fraying at the edges.

It's nearly the way I looked for quite some time after my transformation—pale, but plump, because food was plentiful. My nose, however, has always been long, straight and distinguished (though my mouth, admittedly, lacks some of its youthful fullness, especially since the war ended), and to this day I have no idea how little Luke's nose got that way. Maybe Regina Watson chopped it off.

I had a promising early adulthood, as long as it lasted. I knew I was smarter than my parents and my friends, and smarter than the people at the weekly prayer meetings. They knew it too, and some of them instinctively mistrusted me because of it. But others—gentle, good-natured people—told my father that by God I had to be sent off to *school* I was so smart, and wouldn't it be a *sin against creation* if I didn't get a chance at least to get out of the Kentucky hills. So my father got some money together, I did some extra work for some people in Hanford, and on the day I saw little Luke press his miserably plump face into Regina Watson's window I was just two weeks shy of boarding a train for Louisville. I was going to "ex-spear-ee-ence the big city," my father told me. I looked forward to it. I day-dreamed about it. And when he asked me to go introduce myself to Regina Watson, I was day-dreaming that she'd be the kind of woman I'd want to spend the rest of my life with. She'd be lush and willing and bright (though not, of course, as bright as I), and I'd tell her, "I'm going to *Louisville*. I'm going to live there for awhile," which would impress the hell out of her. And when I got back from Louisville she'd be mine just for the asking because I'd have *ex-spear-ee-ence*. It was a day-dream I'd had often, with variations, about a great many women.

And I think that with respect to Regina Watson, it faded a little when I heard the squeak of her washrag. It was a very telling squeak. It told me that clean windows mattered a great deal to her and, as far as I was concerned, clean windows meant little more than that people could look into your house and know your business.

But when she looked at me and said, "Who are you?" the day-dream returned in force because she was so damned appealing, because I found myself wanting her even before her question was done. Because, I realize now, I saw in her the means of breaking the hard and stifling grip that virginity had on me.

I saw something else, too. I saw the cold and quiet on-rush of panic in her, and it made her seem very vulnerable, which made her seem attainable, even to a virginal and awkward-looking young man who hadn't even been to Louisville.

So, with my friend Lemuel, I went back to her house the next day.

(I liked having Lemuel around, then. I knew he wasn't terribly bright, and there was a wide streak of cruelty in him that surfaced every now and then and made me cringe. But I think that he recognized from the beginning of our relationship that I was his superior in all things, so he was like a kind of very loyal if unpredictable dog. And I found him occasionally entertaining, too. Especially later, after my transformation.)

It was the day that little Luke pressed his miserable face into the window, the day that Lemuel got stung in the temple, and the day I sat down with my murderer. My redeemer. Regina Watson. Who served me home-made corn muffins, and cider, and quick, nervous talk.

"You shouldn'ta been around there," she said, then packed Lemuel's temple in mud and told him to lie down on two, big, threadbare feather pillows she had

75

put in a corner of her kitchen. "You're lucky he didn't come right out the window atcha." Lemuel grinned a big, toothy grin that was half apology and half stupidity. Then she told him, again and again, "You'll be all right, you'll be all right." Her sudden and obvious concern scared the crap out of him and he shook visibly on those pillows, his hand pressed hard to his temple, where the bee had stung him, as if to concentrate on the pain.

She had shown us into her house through a side door that led into the kitchen. The door to the rest of the house was bolted and that interested me because the day was hot and still, so the kitchen, too, was abominably hot. Opening that bolted door would have provided for some circulation of air.

She told me to sit down at the kitchen table—a battered and apparently home-made dark oak table with four chairs that had each obviously been plucked from second-hand stores, or auctions, and out of old houses.

"I must feed you," she said crisply. She wore the same plain white dress I had seen her wearing the day before, and it hung very fetchingly on her. I guessed that it had once belonged to a much taller owner, because it was stitched at the hem with coarse, black thread.

I said, feeling bold, "Is that your boy in the room back there?" I nodded to indicate the room I'd seen Luke in.

"I got no boy," she said. Her lips quivered as she said it and I remember feeling a pang of sympathy for her. "I got the Lord. I got my memories, and I got this

76

house, and I got the Lord. And the Lord says to feed the hungry and to tend to the sick"—meaning Lemuel, who was still shivering on the feather pillows—"and send them on their way."

"Sure," I said. "Sure, I'm awful hungry," which was a lie, but if she wanted to feed me, I was more than willing to let her. I looked at Lemuel. "Hey, Lemuel, you're hungry, ain'tcha?"

Regina Watson nodded earnestly. "We are all of us hungry, Mr Land. For one thing or another." It pleased me that she remembered my name. "And food's just a small part of it. Some of us got a hunger of the soul."

I said, trying to keep up my end of the conversation, "And who might that be? Who might have a hunger of the soul, M's Watson?"

She went to one of her cupboards—they had, I guessed, once been attractive oak and glass, but most of the glass was gone, except for shards jutting out from several corners, and the oak had been poorly stripped of an off-white paint because there were gouges everywhere in it—and she brought back a pie-tin covered with waxed paper. She took the waxed paper off, folded it neatly in half, put it on the table, held the pie-tin out to me. "Take one, please," she said. "They're fresh-made just yesterday mawnin'."

She stuck the corn muffins directly under my nose. They had a vaguely rancid odor about them, but not so much, I guessed, that they'd make me sick, so I took one, smiled gratefully, took a bite of it. "Thanks," I said as I chewed. "Thanks, Miss Watson." (I still remember that vaguely rancid smell. I like the memory; it's something sweet, because smells don't come to me anymore. Not even the smell of the dead all around, for which I am thankful, and not the smell of hollyhocks and irises and primroses, which seem to bloom in abundance here, and not the smell of my own corruption, which, I've been told by several of my victims, is something less than pleasant.)

In life, in fact, I was extremely susceptible to smells. If a smell was enjoyable, I did very much enjoy it. It was, possibly, an almost sexual enjoyment (as, I think, the vaguely rancid smell of those corn muffins was, considering who had served them to me, and what my intentions were in being at her house). But if a smell was bad—like the smell of the various small animals that our cats stored under the porch of the house on Phillips Road—then I was not merely repulsed, I was often made physically ill. And that's why I don't miss too much the *living* sense of smell that left me eighty years ago. Now, all my senses—my sight, my hearing, my sense of touch—have become as much the senses of the living creatures all around me as my own. I see through the eyes of insects and mice and birds as much as through my own eyes. And occasionally, I see through *his* eyes, too.

I don't believe that Regina Watson knew she was destined to be my murderer. She firmly believed herself capable of keeping and feeding a young vampire, as if he were merely a raccoon, or a white mouse. But it was a task that had clearly taken its toll on her. Sitting in her kitchen, being near enough to her to judge, I could see that she had gone without sleep for several nights. Her eyes were puffy and bloodshot, and gray folds of skin sagged beneath them.

"What happened to him?" I asked, and again indicated the room I'd seen Luke in.

She went to a squat, oak cupboard near the door to the rest of the house, opened the cupboard, withdrew a chipped white enamel pitcher, brought it back to the table, set it down hard, and said again, with a trace of anger, "I got no boy, Mr Land."

I decided to shut up. She was a woman with much on her mind, I realized, and I was just a boy she'd caught doing what he should not have been doing.

She went back to the oak cupboard, got a blue plastic cup, brought it back to the table, and poured the cider into it. "Here," she said, "drink this," and handed me the cup. I took it. She sat down. To my right, on the feather pillows, Lemuel began to snore.

She sat kitty-corner to me at the table, folded her hands on top of it, and said very quickly, eyes averted, as if it were a painful thing to say, "The creature's name is Luke and he is cursed." She was looking at one of the two windows that overlooked the porch just off the kitchen—both were open, and a fitful breeze that I could not feel was pushing two sets of soiled, white flower-print curtains about. "He strayed from the Lord, and from me, Mr Land, and he is cursed—the Lord has cursed him, and *I* have cursed him."

"Call me Elmo," I said, and she looked offended. "Elmo," I repeated, and sipped at the apple cider in an attempt to put both of us at ease.

"Are you a believer?" she asked.

I admitted fumblingly that I wasn't.

"Oh," she said, as if I had taken her by surprise.

"Oh," she said again, as if her surprise had quickly become embarrassment. She looked hard at me. "Then I don't know why I'm talking to you, Mr Land," she said, and scooped up the pie-tin filled with corn muffins, the pitcher full of warm cider, even the blue plastic cup, put them all frantically away, went over to where Lemuel had fallen asleep, and gave him a short, sharp kick that landed on his knee. He woke at once, shrieking, though from where I sat the kick had not looked hard enough to elicit shrieking. "Get up, you!" she commanded. "Get up!"—kick—"Get up!" But he was standing, and shrieking, even as she continued to kick him.

"I'm up!" he screeched. "Shit, I'm up!" and moments later he was out the side door, shrieking again.

3

The war started not quite one year ago, on April 11th. It started the way all wars start. Someone wanted something that someone else had and rather than ask for it he grabbed for it. His reasons were sensible enough. His people were in need, and their former high standard of living had declined dramatically due to forces over which he had absolutely no control. So he reached out and tried to take what he needed from one of his neighbors. It wouldn't really have done him much good to ask, *everyone* a year ago April 11th was in need, and no one's standard of living was then what it once had been. Still, he should have asked. It would have been the civilized thing to do. But he chose to grab, and he got his hand slapped. He pouted for a couple of weeks, and while he pouted he spewed forth an endless volley of recriminations and accusations and vile threats. But no one took him seriously, even though he was crazy (*everyone* had said so time and time again, but, I think, with a kind of grudging admiration, as if he were somehow monstrously *cute*). He also let it be known that he had gotten hold of some very nasty weapons from some-where. Some said from the Soviets, some said from the Americans, still others said from the British, and a few others asked what the hell difference it made.

He used the weapons on April 11th against the neighbor from whom he had so desperately tried to grab what he needed. The neighbor, it turned out, had also gotten some nasty, illicit weapons from some-where, saw what was coming and cut loose with them. They were, as luck would have it, the nuclear equivalent of Saturday night specials. Most of them blew up in his face, only two of them made it anywhere near their target, and the other one found its way to an obscure oil sheikdom. Until that moment, the war might have remained a more-or-less private squabble between two madmen, and per-haps the world's living might have been much better off without them, too. But when that small oil sheik-dom got hit and the world's TVs were filled with images of millions upon millions of barrels of oil going up in smoke, the cry of "conspiracy" rose up and quickly became deafening.

That's when the war got incredibly stupid.

I had been spending my days in an abandoned fruit-stand near a town called Friend, in upstate New York. I had been to all the eastern states and I liked New York, especially its small, rural communities, like Friend, because people tended to mind their own business—at least, they had business of their own to mind. They were bright, they had hobbies, and they belonged to various organizations—the PTA, the Grange, et cetera—which was not true of rural people everywhere, and certainly wasn't true of city people. I had, in fact, struck up a passing acquaintance with several of the people in Friend, who were certain that I had bought one of the several dozen abandoned farms that had gone up for sale there in the last couple years. I like to think that some of those people survived the war, even though, it's true, several of their sons and daughters became my willing victims. And I suppose that if those people did not survive, and if they, like the people in this village, are lying about in pain, they would have to forgive me now because they must see that nothing I did to them at all compares to what they finally did to themselves.

4

Regina Watson came to our house on the night she
threw Lemuel and me out of hers. She was shaking
just as violently as Lemuel had, and she was clutching
a number of religious ornaments in her hands, which
my father and mother found extremely interesting
because they were Baptist and had probably never
seen a crucifix, or a St Christopher medal, two of the
items Regina Watson was clutching.

They ushered her into the house at once, being
good, generous, hill people, sat her down at the
kitchen table—a white enamel drop-leaf my father
had picked up at auction for two dollars—got her hot
coffee, and a fresh sourdough biscuit. Then each of
them sat kitty-corner to her. I remember watching
from the living room, where I'd been sent by my
mother with the words, "I'm sure this is none of your
business, Elmo." (She was a stout woman, tall, and
very strong. I remember that I felt great affection for
her, but I recall her now only vaguely, as if she is
some kind of rotund cartoon character: her words, in
my memory—a memory which has been grotesquely

altered by what I've become—appear in little word-balloons, and her voice is mechanical, not quite human.)

Regina spoke loudly, in a low tenor falsetto that was clearly the result of her fear, and I could hear her perfectly. She ignored the coffee and biscuit, lowered her head and spoke to the crucifix and the St Christopher medal.

"Forgive me, oh forgive me," she said.

My father touched her wrist lightly, "Certainly we will, Mrs Watson."

"Elmo, let her speak!" my mother scolded. Then, to Regina, "Tell us what you've done." She made no attempt to camouflage the fact that it was a command.

Regina, however, was clearly not going to be intimidated. She said, still as if to the crucifix and St Christopher medal, her voice stiff, "You are in grave danger. I'm sorry, I am so sorry, but you are all in very grave danger."

My mother took a quick, agitated breath. My father grinned his *Aren't-my-teeth-beautiful!* grin, patted Regina's wrist again—he seemed to enjoy touching her—and said very soothingly, "Thank you for coming to tell us that . . ."

And my mother cut in, her voice strident, "Shush your mouth, Elmo. Just shush your mouth." He did as he was told.

I giggled, caught my mother's quick, threatening look, put my hand to my mouth, and turned away. "And you too, Elmo Junior," she said.

I heard Regina Watson push herself to her feet. I

looked at her and saw that she had both ends of the crucifix in a white-knuckled death grip, and that her eyes were open very wide. Then the crucifix snapped. My mother gasped. Regina Watson looked down, open-mouthed, at the two ends of the crucifix dangling from her hands, then up at my father, who was grinning once again, then at my mother, who for once was completely at a loss for words. Then she let out the most hair-raising, maniacal, and hellish scream I have ever heard—even since my transformation, and I have heard some incredibly hellish screams since then—and, still screaming, vaulted from the house.

My mother said, after a long moment of silence, "Woman's got toys in her attic, I'm thinkin'!" But there was no conviction in her voice. She was plainly scared. My father said, "Woman's crazy as a bedbug." There was fear in his voice, too, and it scared me. He looked at my mother. "That woman's crazy as a bedbug, Myrna, she's 'bout went over the edge."

That was the last thing said about Regina Watson that night.

Lemuel and I went back to her house early the following morning. It was a cool morning, alive with the twitterings and chirpings of morning birds.

We took a route that led us through a stand of piney woods behind Regina's house because we intended to spy on her. She was the news of the year in Hanford, as far as we were concerned. She was more fun than watching a rabid fox, Lemuel said. Maybe she'd tear her clothes off and run around naked, he said, which was an idea I found incredibly appealing.

Lemuel was wearing blue overalls that morning. No shirt, no underwear—he never wore underwear—and hand-me-down brown shoes, *sans* socks, that were a size too large so they added considerably to his clumsiness. He'd also found a much-used corn cob pipe, which he stuck unlit into his mouth. This was the Huck Finn kind of costume he affected during all the decades of our relationship.

He's gone, now. The years brought him intelligence of a sort, and, with it, ambition. He started to think about his remaining years, and at last told me that he couldn't see much of a future in continuing to act as a kind of slavering valet to a creature like me, who, of course, had no future at all. That was near Dundotton, Maryland, in 1958. He told me that he was going to sell used cars.

Regina, it turned out, was not running around naked that morning. She was asleep—or so Lemuel and I believed. We could see her through a break in her kitchen curtains, which had been drawn together. She was on her back on the feather pillows—where she'd put Lemuel the day before—with her arms at her sides, her legs straight, her off-white dress arranged so it flared out left and right at her ankles.

"She's sleepin'," Lemuel whispered. "Elmo, she's sleepin'."

We had already gone around to the window where poor Luke had appeared but when we looked in we saw only a narrow, wrought-iron bed, a stained mattress, and a pile of crap—Luke's, I assumed—in a far corner. The door to the room was open, too, and through it we could see something of what looked like a parlor—the edge of a big, dark upright piano, what appeared to be a bluish oriental rug, the front edges of a delicate, red couch with white doilies on the arms.

Lemuel asked, "We at the right house, Elmo?"

"We are," I told him. It seemed to ease his apprehension because he gave me one of his long, ear-to-ear grins. They were grins which announced that at that moment in his life he was immensely contented, nothing was amiss, all questions had been answered. It was at such times that I felt something like affection for him, the same way that people feel affection for an especially malleable and eager-to-please dog. After my transformation, of course, that affection changed to anger, and more than a few times I had to draw on some lingering traces of humanity to keep from tearing his throat out.

We did not linger at Regina Watson's kitchen window. I felt uneasy there, as if the house had been slowly filling up with gas all night and would soon explode. "Lemuel," I said, "maybe we'd better go." This took a moment to sink in because he had fully expected, I think, that we'd do more than peek in a few windows, but at last he said, "Sure," and we started for my home down Phillips Road.

And it was there, on Phillips Road, on the way

home, with my less-than-bright friend Lemuel beside me, that I realized for the first time that I was not going to survive much past the following afternoon.

That I was going to be immortal.

5

———

I had no brothers or sisters. Apparently I gave Ma quite a hard time during labor and delivery. Some time later, my father told me that she almost died, in fact. So they never entertained the idea of having more kids, though having kids was a much-loved pastime in the Kentucky hills where I grew up.

We had cats, and hound dogs—because all true hill people have hound dogs—and we had a succession of wild animals that my father took in and tried valiantly to tame—skunks, bobcats, we even had a rattlesnake, although it tried for my mother's ankle and ended up as Sunday dinner, with collard greens and white flour biscuits.

Meals at home are the only tastes I remember. I don't taste blood. I *sense* it on my tongue and I *sense* it moving down my throat. But I cannot taste it because my palate is as useless as my lungs, my bowels, and my kidneys. (I remember that a year or so after my transformation, and out of an incredible, strong desperation, I crashed a night-time wedding reception in Louisville. I knew none of the participants. The bride was a fat woman named Edie, her husband a very tall and pitifully gaunt-looking man named Ernest—I knew this because there were lots of toasts to "the health and wealth and happiness of Edie and Ernest". My purpose in crashing the reception was—as the recent phrase has it—to "pig out" on the food. I'd been to several receptions, before my transformation, and had always made a pig of myself, which was expected, so I thought that if I could recreate that aura of gluttony I'd have a toehold, at least, on my absent humanness. I was not without hunger, of course. I had a constant hunger, I still do, but it's a hunger of the soul, and it has no connection whatever with the kind of satisfaction that protein and carbohydrates and fatty acids used to give me.

So, I got into a long line that had formed at one of the buffet tables, got a plate, some silverware, a napkin, and loaded the plate up to overflowing. This was a halfway posh affair, as far as such things went in Louisville, and, in retrospect, I think loading my plate up like that was my undoing—everyone else was taking very small, even dainty portions. So when the man behind me—one of the groom's relatives, I'm sure, because he was also tall and gaunt-looking—saw that my plate was heaped high, he said, "Bit much there, boy. This isn't the back woods; you brought up in a barn, or what?"

Probably because of some lingering human pride, I took offense at that. I said stiffly, "No. I grew up in the house my father built," and realized at once that I shouldn't have opened my mouth at all, for several reasons—the most important being that the tone of my voice is hugely sepulchral, theatrically sepulchral, a basso profundo sepulchral, and when I said what I said a number of people turned their heads sharply and looked in awe at me. One of them, a young, burly man, asked, "Who the hell are you?"

"No one." I answered, which, I realized sadly, was very much the truth. "I'm hungry," I added, which was also the truth, though, again sadly, I knew that I was hungry for something other than what was being served there.

"I don't believe that you were invited to this affair," said the same man, his voice quivering now.

"The door was open," I said.

"It still is," said the same man. "And it works just as well as an exit."

The chances were that I could have wreaked considerable havoc—the truth is, I very much wanted to wreak considerable havoc because, in large part, the asshole in line behind me had pissed me off. But there were at least two hundred and fifty people there, fully half of them men, and though it is true that, as a species, vampires are incredibly strong, they're not supermen, and they're not stupid, either. "I'm sorry," I said. "I'll see you around," and I left.

I had girlfriends in Hanford—not a lot of them but enough so that I knew what females looked like and felt like at a pretty early age. Hanford was a very small village. At its peak, in the first decade of the twentieth century, it boasted a little over five hundred inhabitants, most of whom, if asked, would have called themselves farmers or carpenters. They had settled in Hanford for various reasons—because their parents had settled there, and their parents before them, et cetera, et cetera, or because they had been chased out of some other little town where the people in power were big on morality, or because, simply, Hanford was a pretty place nestled in a pretty valley.

I don't think that anyone would want to drop bombs on it, so I imagine that it's still a pretty place. Perhaps I'll go and see one of these days, if I can find my way back. (It's something my friend, Lewis Perdue, did after his transformation. He went back to his boyhood home; he had been drawn there, he said.

(His home was on a beach near Falmouth, Massachusetts. He went there, he said, "to get it all back". I had no idea what he was talking about, and I said so. "Get what back?" I asked.

("Only what's important," he said.

(Apparently he didn't find what he was looking for because he went back home for only a week or so.

(He taught the night class in English Literature. He was a very strange duck. He said to me once, "So what are you going to do afterward, Elmo?"

("Afterward?" I said.

(He nodded. "After it's all done. After it stops making any sense."

("Sense?" I laughed. "It doesn't need to make sense, Lewis."

(I think I could still laugh at him.

(But I do miss him.)

*

My girlfriends in Hanford were named Lorna, Rebecca, Katherine, and Hope: I remember none of their last names—and any one of them could have kept me from dying a virgin. None of them were virgins, except Hope, and she was ugly. But none of them made that effort, they wanted *me* to, and I was a coward. I was ignorant, sexually, I was small, also sexually, so I had no confidence whatsoever. (I sought out one of those girlfriends, Rebecca, a few months after my transformation, hoping that my new . . . persona would enable me to perform at last. It didn't. I wasn't interested in her, she wasn't interested in me. I succeeded only in scaring the hell out of her, and I went away from her house feeling pity for myself, and anger, emotions which are quite magnified in me now.)

So I died a virgin.

Regina Watson came to me the night after Lemuel and I saw her on the feather pillows in her kitchen. My bedroom was on the first floor of the house on Phillips Road, and in summer I left the window wide open, without a screen, and, as anyone well-versed in vampire lore knows, open windows are the equivalent of an engraved invitation. *Come right in*, they say. *Do with me what you will.*

So Regina Watson did.

She did not float in. Vampires can't float. They're bound by most of the physical laws that bind the living.

She stepped in, over the sill, her left leg first, then

her right, that long off-white dress hiked up to mid-thigh. A waning gibbous moon cast a cool and sultry glow on her.

She looked hungry. We all have that look about us. We can't shed it because we're constantly hungry. But she looked fetching, too. As thin as she was, and as hungry as she was.

I could not see her eyes well because of the darkness in them, the shadow of her brow.

I said, "Hi," and added after a pause of several seconds, "Hi, Mrs Watson."

She nodded at me and I saw the glint of her eyes, an off-white like the color of her dress, off-white and cool. Then she turned to her right, went down to the foot of my bed, around it to my right side, and bent over me.

I was a bit put off at first by her smell. I said to her, at a whisper, "Jees, Mrs Watson, what you been doin'?" because she smelled as if she'd been handling dead animals. Then it occurred to me that she might have been preparing possum, or raccoon, and had merely forgotton to clean herself up. "Sorry," I said, because I thought I was being abominably rude, and if she was giving me the chance to shed my virginity, I was in no position to question why she smelled the way she did.

She was still holding her dress up. She said, "Hello, Mr Land," and chuckled. It was coarse, and humorless, but to be polite I smiled at her. I said once again, "Hi, Mrs Watson," and added, "Whatchoo doin' here?" because, of course, I wanted her to *tell* me what she was doing. I wanted her to say, "I want you," because, she'd taken the initiative in coming to my bedroom, so I wanted her to keep the initiative all the way to the end. What did I know? I was a virgin, after all.

So she said, "I want you, Mr Land."

"You do?" I said, and smiled again.

"Come, come, Mr Land," she whispered. It was an invitation. "Give me yourself."

My father pushed the door open then. We had no electricity in the house and he was carrying a kerosene lamp. He held it out so the room was lit by it. "Holy jumpin' Jehosophat, Elmo!" he declared.

Regina Watson was still bent over me. She turned her head very slowly, saw my father. "Get out!" she hissed.

He smiled. "Sure," he said. "Sure, Mrs Watson." He looked at me. His smile became conspiratorial. "Good boy, Elmo," he said. "Good boy!" Because he was convinced I was in the process of losing my virginity. "Jus' don't make too much noise, okay, 'cuz we don't want your ma waking up."

I could say nothing to him. In a moment he turned and left the room, still smiling conspiratorially.

And Regina Watson lay on top of me then, a small sniffling noise coming from her, as if she had a cold, and I could see the moonlight dancing on the skin of her arms and thighs, and her brow shadowing her eyes again . . .

I am very stimulated by this.

Sunday

Her skin felt like the skin of a carrot just plucked from the earth as her fingers slid over me, and I realized that she wasn't sniffling. It was something else, something her lips did. It was the same kind of thing that the living do in anticipation of something tasty.

And when her lips were on me I thought of the way that hogs eat because that was the sound I heard from her, a sound I make, too, when I feed. And as she fed, I heard my father call softly, from beyond the door, "Good boy, Elmo!"

At last, she got up, stepped back, hesitated, said one word—"More!"—moved very gracefully to the window, put her right leg up, over the sill, then her left, dress up to mid-thigh, and was gone.

6

_____

We read minds. Not always clearly, or well, especially
when there are thousands and thousands of them
working, as in cities—which I've always tried to stay
away from—and especially during the day, when
minds are particularly active (and that is one of the
key reasons we operate at night—to avoid the clutter
of so many minds working at once. The sun, also, has
proved to be bothersome to us, not because it is the
living symbol of purity or light or goodness—it isn't—
but because we are an anaemic, fair-skinned species,
so we tend to burn easily.)

I can read *his* mind now. I know that he's watching
me and that he longs to know who I am, and what I
am. I know that his name is Jeff, that he despises
"Jeffery", his given name, that he misses his Chevrolet
Camaro and wishes he had it here with him.

He misses his dog, too. He named it "Hobo" because
it apparently had the looks of a hobo (and I suppose
that if it had been gray he would have named it
"Smoke"—and that if he'd ever married and had had

a child—which he didn't—he would have named the child "Jeff junior").

I'm going to talk with him. I *need* desperately to talk to *someone*.

Tuesday

Regina Watson did not kill me that night. It's true that the process began then, but when I woke the following morning at close to noon I felt exactly as if I had a hang-over—which, thanks to my father and his whiskey, I'd first experienced at the age of ten, and went on to experience at least two times a week until my death. My father, coming back from his still with a dozen full bottles in a bushel basket saw me come out onto the porch. He gave me another big conspiratorial grin, winked and whispered, "Won't tell your ma nothin'. Proud of you, Elmo." I nodded dumbly and went straight back into the house to get out of the sunlight.

I had the bite marks, of course. They felt like smallpox lesions, and they itched terribly. There were two of them, not quite three inches apart, in a line on my right jugular. Regina had been wonderfully precise.

I wanted her terribly. I was beginning to learn what compulsion and obsession were (because these are the things which animate us) and I didn't much care for it. I liked having *reasons* for what I did. Lemuel was my closest friend, I knew, because I could dominate him. I was a virgin, I knew, because I lacked confidence in myself, and because most women intimidated me. As Regina Watson did. But still I wanted her. I could think of nothing else but her. And when Lemuel came to the house at a little past noon— "Gawd, Elmo," he said, "somethin' bitcha there ya know!"—I started for her house, down Phillips Road, and he followed, though I was barely aware of him.

And when I got there, I went directly in, through the kitchen door, as if the house were mine, and I sought her out on the feather pillows.

She appeared to be sleeping, though I sensed, with my eyes on her and my need for her, that "sleeping" was not the right word at all, and it made my desire and my obsession even greater.

"You oughta not be in here, Elmo," Lemuel said behind me. I whirled around and grabbed him by the collar and pulled him close—he was taller than I, but not quite as heavy, though it would have made no difference if he was—and I snarled at him, "Get out of here, Lemuel! And don't let me see you again until I want you!" I pushed him away. He stared at me, dumbfounded, for several seconds, then stumbled out.

To the right of where Regina Watson lay, on the feather pillows, and about five feet from her, a closed, bolted door led to the cellar. Something was scratching on the other side of that door, much as a cat does, and, as I listened to it, Regina Watson's eyes popped open, a look of quick panic passed over her, then her eyes closed.

A long shuddering breath came from her. After a moment, I realized that she was attempting to speak.

I said, with a nervous quiver in my voice, "Regina?"

I waited a moment, repeated it: "Regina?" She fell silent.

It was Luke, of course, scratching at the other side of that door, trying to get back to his mother, moaning deep within himself, as if to tell her how very sorry he was for having been a naughty boy. I could feel it, I could *hear* it, just as I was hearing the birds outside Regina's open windows. It was the same kind of sound that a mole makes when it pushes through the earth, the sound that an iris makes when it opens, the *same* sound, for the *same* reasons—to survive—the same pathetic sound that Regina Watson made there on her feather pillows, a sound that was survival itself, a sound that declared so clearly her need to survive, her passion to *be*.

And it didn't matter at all what she was.

(It is the same sound, in fact, that these people here—all lying around dead and in pain—are making, a sound that declares that *they* wouldn't mind being what *I* am, as long as they could *be*, as long as they could *survive*.)

And Regina, on her feather pillows, still smelled the way she had the night before, as if she'd been processing dead animals, but it didn't put me off now. I enjoyed it, I found it stimulating.

This is my birth I'm remembering.

I wanted to get close to that smell, close to her. I saw her eyes pop open, I saw panic in them again, but I saw something else too—recognition.

She smiled crookedly at me, as if she had great difficulty smiling, then she stood and took me once more. I listened to her feed.

It was that sound, *her* sound. It was the last sound I heard.

Near midnight, I went back to the house on Phillips Road, and when I went into my bedroom I became aware that I had changed inalterably.

Wednesday

Jeff wants to call out to me and ask who I am. He wants companionship and says to himself again and again that he's lonely. He pities himself, and believes that he's weak and unmasculine for it.

If I call out to him I'll spook him because he wants to make the first move, wants to surprise me, in fact (and wouldn't *that* be a trick), because he thinks I lack for companionship, too. But I have the dead all around, who talk to me, in their way.

And I must be very careful with this man. He doesn't think much of himself, he think she's a nebbish—a word that rattles around in his head. He thinks he's ineffectual, and he feels very confused because he survived the war while so many millions of others didn't.

But I feel something else in him, too. Something I have felt in others. A kind of patient and growing strength, as if gallons and gallons of adrenalin are waiting for release.

7

Saturday

He's burying the dead. They plead with him not to, but he can't hear them, of course. He supposes that he's being moral—the phrase "A good, Christian burial" goes through his head like a song, and occasionally a little tune creeps in with it, so he has begun devising lyrics for it: "Gonna give 'em a good Christian burial, a good Christian burial, a *good* Christian burial," is about as far as he's got.

He is the soul of confusion. Try as he might, he can't understand why *he* survived the war. He even lightly entertains the idea that he's been "chosen" somehow, which gives him a twinge of pride that he chases away at once because he thinks of himself as humble and self-effacing.

But he's scared. He's scared of the war and of the shit it left behind. He's scared of the dead, scared of himself. He doesn't like that. He needs to be in control, he believes he has always *been* in control. Poor slob.

And he has planned tomorrow as the day he will announce himself to me. It's a special day for him, the

20th of April. Several decades ago he did something vaguely heroic on the 20th of April, and he has been convinced ever since that it's *his* day.

He knew a woman here, in this village. Her name was 'Lizbeth, and he remembers her body especially. He doesn't *like* that. He'd prefer to believe that her body was only of secondary importance to him, and it is with great reluctance that he admits she had precious little else to offer *except* her body.

He came here, to Mumford, in search of her. She lived at number 26 Vine Street. End of the block. A dead end. And her house is still there (most of them are, though a few have been burned by vandals). It's a big fieldstone monster in need of a roof; it has a For Sale sign stuck in the middle of the front lawn.

He found 'Lizbeth's mother in a downstairs parlor. She was seated forever in a cane-back rocker with knitting needles on her lap and a ball of light green yarn trailed across the room—probably, he decided, the result of the family cat's playfulness.

He found 'Lizbeth's father on his back in a tool shed at the rear of the house, a Black and Decker three by eight inch drill clutched to his chest.

And although these were pathetic discoveries, Jeff thought they were also somehow touching, even if the stench of death was everywhere.

He imagines that he's in some kind of movie. He even entertains fantasies of giving the human race a new start—he as the father and 'Lizbeth as the mother, and I want to yell at him, "Hey, wise up, it's not going to happen. You're my lunch, you're ham and cheese on rye, you're Fritos, a cold glass of Coke, a crisp salad!"

He's found a house to live in. It's two blocks down from 'Lizbeth's—because he believes she might come back one day—and it doesn't have the stench of death in it because the people who owned it were on vacation when the war started.

He found a transistor radio, listened to the white noise of static for a good half-hour, then turned it off to save the batteries.

He desperately wants to live, and I'd pity him if I could, if he wasn't doing enough of it already for both of us.

Night. I found one of the townies still alive and had my fill, stuffed her away in a closet for safe-keeping on the off-chance she'd live another day or two, went back several hours later, found that she'd suffocated. I keep forgetting that these creatures need air.

Her name was Dolores and she had red hair and green eyes. Perhaps I should have been gentler with her, maybe I could have kept her somewhere, dined at my leisure on her.

Next time, perhaps.

For now—to sleep.

April 20

Jeff is burning houses. He tells himself that fire *cleanses* after all, that fire *purifies*, and again and again he finds

105

that he's smiling, with his eyes on the flames, because he likes fire (he thinks it's a secret he's successfully kept from the rest of the world all his life). He has lots of secrets—an obsession with women who remind him of his mother, as 'Lizbeth did, a fear of spiders (which he has valiantly tried to overcome), a deep-seated and firmly held belief that he is on the one hand not really worth very much, and on the other that he's quite special, that he has some sort of immense inner strength. He thinks, as well, that he's crazy. He isn't (at least no more crazy, I think, than any one else would be in his position). He's just someone who's burning the village down for the sake of good sanitation.

He's my dinner one of these fine evenings.

At last he has screwed up some courage and shouted to me from across the village square at just past sunset, when there was light enough. "Who are you?" he called. It was the first time I actually heard his voice and not simply his own mental representation of it, which in his head is a charming, soft tenor. Through the air it is close to a squawk. Laryngitis, he thinks.

"My name's Elmo," I called back. "Who are you?"

"My name's Jeff."

"Are you alone, Jeff?"

He thought about that a moment, a quick uneasiness ran through him, and he answered, "Aren't we all?" which he supposed, almost in so many words, was pretty damned profound. "Aren't we all alone?"

I think that I grimaced. It would be nice to believe

that I did—these facial expressions get harder and harder to do as the years progress. I called back, "I saw smoke."

He cleared his throat, swallowed, opened his mouth to speak, closed it, glanced about. At last he said, "Uh-huh." A short pause. "Spontaneous ignition." His voice cracked. "Lightning. It must have been lightning."

I swear that something very close to a chuckle broke from my throat. Across the square, he probably thought it was simply a bad cough because he called urgently, "Are you okay?"

"Yes," I answered. "And you?"

"Fine." He glanced about again, nodded to indicate the town. "I guess we're the only ones left alive, huh?"

"That's possible," I answered.

He considered, then called, "I found a woman. She hadn't been dead very long, less than a day, I think. I wish I'd gotten to her sooner."

"Uh-huh," I called, and immediately felt uneasiness pass through him again. The bastard was reading *me*, though he wasn't aware of it. I added, "That would have been good. We could have shared her." And I felt his uneasiness double and realized my *faux pas*. I went on, "If she'd been alive, I mean," which didn't help at all because he answered, "What'd you say your name was again?"

"Elmo Land."

"Oh. Sure. I'll see you tomorrow, Mr Land." And he turned and jogged back to his little house.

*

I want to talk about my first kill.

I need to talk about my first kill. It stirs something sweet inside me, it stimulates me; I do it all over again, I satisfy that first, wonderful agonizing need and lust all over again, I break that boy's skin and the life beneath rises up and spills over my tongue and into my throat like butter.

I could never taste the blood, though I've always so wanted to.

It was a young boy whose name was George. He lived two miles from the house on Phillips Road and he was coming home late from school and I swept over him with my arms wide and I remember he turned around and began to laugh at me because he thought it was a joke.

Then I tore him up.

And oh I am going to do the very same thing to this man one of these evenings when I'm through with him.

I see through his eyes. I see the lace curtains, the cheap oriental-style vases, the Muntz color TV.

I got an A in anatomy, I got an A in English Literature, an A in Biology. I was damned smart; I still am. Death didn't make me stupid, it just took my breath away.

Jeff is afraid of me. He's scared to death of me, because he's locked himself up in that ugly little house, goddamn him, in the bathroom, and has found a gun somewhere.

Then I threw George into a culvert and I heard his head go *sploosh!*, into a rock, I guess. I didn't bother to look. I still had some feeling for beauty and I knew I had made him look very ugly.

But Dolores is still dead. Jeff took her out of that closet, laid her on the bed, folded her hands on her belly.

She tells me that he *touched* her, but I don't believe her.

And after George there was a creature named Holly who was very fat. I kept her alive and fed on her for weeks. Those were easy times.

I see through Jeff's eyes. I see the Burnwell gas stove, the Kelvinator refrigerator, the dead cat at its bowl of cream which has long since turned to cheese—he throws the cat out the back door, *Put the cat out!* he says. *Put the cat out!*

The man longs for insanity.

I can help him get it.

I can give him an eternity of it, an eternity of drooling into his soup.

I'm a very powerful creature. Much has been written about my power—I move with great speed, I have been insane for eighty years, I killed George and Holly and a thousand others.

In my sleep, in the place I have chosen to sleep, I heard him calling to me, "Mr Land, Mr Land, I'm sorry!" though he had no idea for what. He's lonely, and now that I'm awake he sleeps and he dreams about 'Lizbeth and her enormous breasts.

We do not dream. We can't. This thing called a brain inside our skulls is nothing more than a liquified mass of dead tissue. No current passes through it. It might as well be water (and in some of us who are very old, that's precisely what it is).

In sleep we are free, we become a part of existence—we have no hunger, or memory, or need. We *become* all that *is*. We experience nothing. We experience all.

We are the sow bug underfoot, the stalk of wheat falling to the farmer's blade, the infant routing at its mother's breast, the stack of cumulus that some small boy makes monsters of, a summer leaf, the nose of a poet, mother of pearl.

8

April 21

His first words to me this evening were, "Tell me where you come from."

"Hanford, Kentucky," I told him.

"And how did you survive the war?"

"I was in the right place at the right time."

He nodded. "Me, too." He gave me a once-over. "You look . . . hungry, Mr Land."

I believe that I grinned. "I am," I said. "I think a lot of people are."

He gave me another quick once-over, and a look of concern passed across his face. "Are you in pain, Mr Land?"

"You're very perceptive," I said.

"Is there anything I can do for you?"

"Yes," I answered.

"What?"

"I'll let you know," I said.

We were sitting across from each other in a booth at a restaurant called *Sid's*, near the village square.

He nodded to indicate my polo shirt and my shorts. "Aren't you cold dressed like that?"

"Cold?"

He gestured toward the window. "It can't be more than forty-five or fifty degrees out there."

I noticed that he was wearing a denim jacket.

"Cold has never affected me too very much," I told him. "I'm thick-skinned." He thinks he's a good-looking man. Perhaps he is. Although I long ago lost the ability to appreciate simple physical attractiveness, I can see that his features are even, and symmetrical. His hair is blond, and he wears it short, although not so severely short that his skull defines its contours. His eyes are grayish-blue, and they move quite a lot. I get the idea that he's either afraid of someone, or is just very watchful. He has reason to be both.

He laughed. It was false and annoying and I must have grimaced because he said again, reaching across the table and touching my wrist, "Can I get you something? You look awful. Are you in pain?"

"No. Thank you for your concern," I said.

He withdrew his hand, clasped it in his other hand self-consciously, glanced at the village square again, which was quite dark now, except for the very soft glow of a half-moon thirty degrees above the western horizon. "Damned war was pretty bad," he said, as much to himself as to me. "I lost everyone in it. I even lost my dog."

"Hobo?" I said, and of course it took him completely by surprise.

He asked, "How'd you know that?" A hesitant,

112

suspicious grin flickered across his mouth, as if I were some sort of magician about to explain a trick to him.

I attempted a shrug (it must have looked awfully stiff because I could feel that he wanted to ask yet again if I was in pain) and said as matter-of-factly as I could, "*I* had a dog named Hobo. He *looked* like a hobo, you know—he had short floppy ears and a scruffy gray coat and big, limpid brown eyes—"

Jeff cut in, smiling from ear to ear, "That's *my* dog!" then went on, in a rush, still smiling, "I had a dog just like that, and his name was Hobo, too." His smile altered; he has good teeth, though there are several cavities starting that he's not aware of. "What a damned coincidence, Mr Land—"

"Elmo," I told him.

"Yes," he said, "thank you. Elmo. Call me Jeff." He was letting his guard down. "You know, Elmo, I was a little . . . leery of you, at first."

"Leery of me?" I sounded incredulous.

He grinned, embarrassed. "Foolish, I know. I mean"—*Look at you*, he thought—"I mean, you look . . ."—*emaciated*—"harmless enough."—*Like death warmed over!*—"I mean, what were you before the war? Probably something"—*gentle*—"harmless enough."—*Jesus, he looks awful*—"What were you?" he repeated. "Let me guess—a pharmacist."—*Probably rented himself out on Hallowe'en*—"Something like a pharmacist, am I right, Elmo?"

I shrugged. "Something like that."

"Or maybe a veterinarian. But I'm probably way off base, right?"

"Right."

113

"I thought so. 'Something like a pharmacist' huh?"

"And what were you, Jeff?"

"Me? I was a literary agent."

"Oh?" I said. "That sounds interesting."

"Yes," he said. "It was." He paused, then continued, "Very bad, this war. Very, very bad." He supposed that he sounded vapid; it upset him.

"People are stupid," I said.

"People have always been stupid, Elmo. But they haven't always been suicidal." He liked saying that. "They haven't always been suicidal." He thought, went on with a shrug, "Maybe it was time for a war. Maybe people were bored so they decided to have a war." He supposed that he had latched onto something. A small, self-satisfied grin appeared on his lips. "I mean"—he glanced away, thought again—"I mean, everyone was *bored*, right, so they decided to have a war. Kind of like throwing a party."

I said, "But this time they let other people make their decisions for them."

He said nothing, and, very briefly, I found that I couldn't read him. Then he said, "I was burning some of the houses down, you know."

"I guessed as much."

"Yes," he said.

"You like fire, don't you, Jeff?"

He looked surprised, then nodded sullenly. "But that's not why I did it, of course."

"Of course." I paused. "Why did you do it?"

He thought about that, and again, briefly, somehow closed his mind off to me, which I found annoying. After eighty years I've grown accustomed to reading people, it's become an essential part of my ability to survive, in fact. (I remember in Charleston, in 1932, there was a pair of self-appointed Vampire Hunters after me. One was named Hiram, the other was a young woman named Betty, and they were having the veritable time of their lives chasing me around the city. And I, after my fashion, was having some fun of my own leading them on the chase, leaving bodies everywhere, which was genuinely offensive to them, of course, I could feel it, but it also seemed to stimulate them—I've found that death stimulates lots of people—and at last I decided I was through with the game and I went to a house on Meeting Street.

(It was a very large house that was listed in the National Register of Historic Places, had been built of red brick, and will undoubtedly be standing as long as I.

(I went to a bedroom at the center of the house.

(It was October, the house was in the process of being refurbished after a minor fire had left it smoke-damaged, and there were a few black workmen being bossed around by a white foreman. But I move very quietly, so they had no idea I was there.

(Until, of course, Hiram and Betty showed up, explained who they were and what they were doing— "There's a madman running loose. He thinks he's a vampire, my God, he's already killed twelve people," which was an accurate count, "and we have every reason to believe that he's come here." I watched the white foreman shrug. He assumed incorrectly that Hiram and Betty were from the police, so he told them, "Sure, go ahead and look around. Just let me

115

know if you find him, huh, 'cuz me and these negroes here will beat the holy crap out of him for you." Which did not put him on my list of favorite people.

(Hiram was carrying a wooden stake, and a mallet. The stake was made of dogwood, which is good vampire-killing stock, and I knew that he intended to use it, that he looked forward to using it, in fact, that he had used it at least twice before—once on a demented creature from Raleigh who was indeed *not* a vampire, but merely had vampiric ambitions, and then, three years later, on Regina Watson, who survived because his aim had been poor.

(And they were certain I was there, in that big brick house on Meeting Street because they had powers of their own, and they were equally certain they'd corner me.

(Hiram was a large man, incredibly strong. Betty was quick and smart. And I could read them both so damned well that I knew, even halfway across Charleston, when they were going to sneeze.

(So I let them feel that they had cornered me. I put myself on a big, brass bed in that bedroom just before sunrise, I waited for them to show up with their vampire-killing paraphernalia, and I watched, through their eyes, as they pushed the door open and slipped with wonderful quickness and grace into the room. Betty stepped to one side, Hiram to the other.

(They saw what looked like a corpse on the brass bed, and, essentially, I imagine that they were right—the long, exquisitely skeletal fingers intertwined over the stomach, the legs straight, the light pink eyes partially opened, and the face a wonderful, classic study in what humans find horrible. Not because it *is* horrible, per se. It isn't. But because of what they *believed* about the capabilities of the creature behind it.

(They said nothing to each other, so as to avoid waking me. Hiram nodded to his right, then pointed at Betty, who nodded back, then he pointed at himself, then to his left. I remember he was wearing a St Christopher medal around his neck and it had somehow fallen out the top of his shirt. He tucked it back in and then I let them circle the room. I felt their suppressed excitement, their joy, their mounting anticipation. They thought, in so many words, *We're going to kill the bastard! Jesus, at last we're going to kill the bastard!* I let them get very, very close with their wooden stakes, their crosses and their holy water. And, when they were close enough that they were beginning to stiffen up with tension and excitement, I could sense, at last, that they were *expecting* me to take them by surprise, *expecting* me suddenly to come awake and tear them apart.

(So that's precisely what I did. Because their expectations were no match at all for my speed and strength and my compulsions. I said to Betty, "You can't second guess us, Betty." And I felt such wonderful, paralytic fear and panic from her because she realized with shrill clarity that her death was only moments away.)

"It's very cleansing," Jeff said. "Fire is very cleansing. It purifies."

"Yes, it does that," I said.

"I think there might be . . . diseases. From the dead," he went on, clearly reaching for the proper rationale. "I *was* burying them . . ."

117

"I know you were."

A small, lop-sided, self-pitying grin appeared on his face. "But it was very hard, very, very hard. I've never done it before. Only with pets, but it's not the same." Another smile, one of embarrassment. "It's not at all the same. People are . . ."

"Bigger?" I offered.

The idea offended him, but he hid it well. "Well, yes, they *are* bigger, of course." He shrugged out of his denim jacket—embarrassment was making him warm and uncomfortable. He wore a blue cowboy shirt beneath the jacket, the kind, I knew, that he never would have worn before the war, and which now— though he gestured at it and said something about it being the only thing available—was clearly something he had always wanted to wear. "People *are* bigger," he repeated. "And they have souls, of course."

"Yes, they do."

"So you have to give them a good, decent burial. A Christian burial."

"If you're so inclined."

This interested him. "You aren't?" he asked.

"To the contrary," I said. "My beliefs are very strong. Stronger than I like, in fact." And I felt a moment's unease sweep over him because he had no idea what I was talking about.

He likes to be in control. He *needs* to be in control. And he knew that at that table, at *Sid's* post-apocalyptic restaurant, in Mumford, New York, no one was in control anymore, except those that were strongest.

And of the two of us, that was me.

9

Jeff believes, with an odd mixture of pride and humil-
ity, that we are among the last intelligent creatures
alive on the planet. It's a presumptuous belief, but
forgivable, because he knows that if it's true it carries
with it a certain high duty to be a good and noble
representative of his all-but-extinct species. And I
suppose that he is. All by himself, he's nothing special.
He's bright, but no genius, wholesome, but not too
wholesome, normally clear-headed, but properly
bemused and befuddled by all that's happened. On
balance, I'd say he's a damned fine representative of
his species, and if the world had been populated by
people like him—instead of by the very bright and the
very stupid, by the very moral and the incredibly
amoral—then April 11th would have come and gone
like any other day.

But it didn't.

I think that I've been a decent representative of my
own species as well. For the sake of us all, I've tried to
keep a "low profile" (as the recently popular phrase
has it). I have been told by creatures who have

survived a hell of a lot longer than I, and who have had access to creatures older still, that we are as old as mankind. We can't be much older. There were, in fact—and this may simply be a nice, romantic myth— *Neanderthal* vampires, pitiful, short-lived beasts who were slaves to what they had become and literally stuffed themselves into oblivion.

We have evolved, since then, because man has evolved.

(We sprang from his hatred, from his lusts and compulsions. We were spontaneous. We grew out of cold nights and dull fires. So we are no *less* than man.)

Wednesday

I've been sleeping here in Mumford in the cellar of a large cobblestone farmhouse a mile from the village square. The house once belonged to a woman named Tad Hamilton, and I can feel that she left only days before the war began, but not that she became a victim of the war.

At night I go through her house and I sort out the memories she left here.

Her memories are knife-edged. They slice the air and make ghosts of themselves that speak and laugh. She had several lovers and I can *smell* their perspiration, and know their smiling insincerity.

She had one hand only, her right, the left amputated after an accident, and so she used a prosthesis, was exceedingly good and gentle with it, could stroke with it, caress with it. She was dark-haired. She had green eyes.

Jeff left me a note that I found on the front door of the house after waking. The note read, "We must talk again, Elmo."

I found him in the little house he had taken for himself, two blocks from 'Lizbeth's house. It was well past sunset. The moon was at half and its light was fluid and cream-colored. He came to the door, smiled, ushered me in. He was wearing a herringbone tweed sports coat, black slacks, black Oxfords, a beige shirt. He thought that he looked very appealing, and he wished that 'Lizbeth were there to see him.

He had made coffee for us. "I rigged up a canister of propane to the gas stove," he said. "I'll bet you haven't had a cup of hot coffee in a long time, Elmo."

I have never had a cup of hot coffee. In Hanford, eighty years ago, whiskey took the place of it.

I took the cup from him, sat in a Mediterranean-style chair with it, spilled it onto my lap, said I was sorry.

"Are you okay, Elmo?" he said. "You look a little shaky."

"I'm fine," I answered.

He smiled politely, excused himself, went into the kitchen, got a towel, brought it back, handed it to me. "Here," he said. I took it; he took my cup. "I'll get you another one, Elmo."

"No," I said. "Thanks. I'm not thirsty."

He looked offended.

"Just half a cup, then," I said, and attempted a smile. He went and got me half a cup of coffee.

"Are you in pain, Elmo?" he said as he handed it to me. "You look like you're in pain."

"I'm always in pain," I said.

"Oh? Arthritis?"

I nodded.

"Gee, that's too bad."

"We all have our crosses to bear," I said, and wished that he could appreciate the joke because I thought it was a good one.

"Where?" he asked, and because again, very briefly, I couldn't read him, I asked, "Where what?"

"Where do you have the arthritis? In your legs, in your wrists? I had an aunt who had it in her elbows." He touched his left elbow with his right hand. "She couldn't unlock her arms—she walked around with her arms straight." He straightened his arms. "Like this, Elmo, like a zombie, sort of." He grinned. "So where do you have yours?"

"In my wrists," I said. "And my hands. My jaw, too. It hurts quite a lot." Then I poured some of the coffee down my throat. I felt nothing at all except a slight tickling sensation that was not unpleasant. So I did it again. Moments later, I felt a tickling sensation between my legs and I realized that—like one of those awful Baby Wet dolls—the coffee had passed directly through me and was trickling out onto the chair.

Jeff looked away, embarrassed. I dabbed at the flow

with the towel, got most of it up, said, "Have you been burning any more houses down?"

He glanced at the stain on the chair. "Not yet," he said, suddenly nervous. He sat cross-legged, with his cup of coffee in hand, on a miserable-looking Mediterranean-style couch nearby. He looked awkward and uncomfortable. "Not yet," he repeated. "I've been . . . preparing a place."

"Oh?"

He inclined his head to the left. "Over that way a couple of blocks." 'Lizbeth's house. "I've been bringing bodies to it." He lowered his head, closed his eyes. He was clearly uncomfortable now. He looked up, sipped delicately at his coffee, grimaced. "Gee, this is horrible, I'm sorry, Elmo. The coffee must have been stale."

"No problem," I said.

He put the coffee cup on the floor near his feet. "I've been bringing bodies to that house," he repeated. "They're everywhere, you know—the bodies, I mean."

"Well they would be, wouldn't they?" I said. It offended him; he seems to take offense quite easily.

"Yes," he said, "they are. And, God, they stink!" He wrinkled his nose up. "But I've gotten most of them, I think. I even found someone in the church, kind of an odd place to die, but I put him there, too, in that house. I'll burn it tomorrow. I've got a few more to collect—"

"A few more?"

"Bodies."

"Oh." I paused, as if for reflection, went on, "This makes you uncomfortable, doesn't it?"

He fidgeted on the couch. "Of course it does," he said, rose, went quickly to the picture window across the room, and stood at it with his back to me. He fancied that he presented a grimly romantic figure there, at the window, hands clasped behind him. "It's necessary work, though," he said, his tone low and meditative.

"Necessary?" I asked.

He nodded sagely. "Sweep out the old, bring in the new—" He stopped, took quick stock of himself, found it difficult to recognize what he was seeing. "And there's the matter of disease, too, of course."

"Yes," I said.

He said nothing, and again I found it very difficult to read him.

"Is something wrong, Jeff?"

"I can't see you," he said. "I'm looking at the reflection of the room in the window here and I can't see you, all I can see is the chair you're sitting in. Why can't I see you, Elmo?"

"You can," I said. And because I have become very, very good at suggestion these past eighty years, in a moment he *could* see me. He smiled.

"Yes," he said. "I can. I'm sorry."

"No need."

After a moment, he went on, "What was I talking about, Elmo?"

"About collecting bodies," I told him.

"Was I? Gee, that's awful."

And at last I realized why I've been having occasional difficulty reading him. There's something else pushing into his brain, and he doesn't know quite what to do with it because it's foreign to what he thinks of himself (he thinks of himself as a man with certain strengths and certain weaknesses, someone who likes fire, and remembers making love to 'Lizbeth, and who tried very hard, often despite himself, to do what is right and moral). But this something else pushing into his brain confuses him and makes him lose track of himself. He doesn't know what to do with it, of course. He wants to get rid of it, but it's incredibly strong, and he likes that—he says to himself that it's *his* strength.

Maybe it is. I'm not sure.

I think I'll keep a closer eye on him.

10

Lemuel and I did our first kill together a week or so after my encounter with Regina Watson.

I made my way to his house—it was a mile from mine, down a narrow dirt road that branched off Phillips Road—and I tapped at his bedroom window. He woke slowly, and when he saw me he shrieked.

He had assumed that I was dead, that Regina Watson had killed me (because everyone knew that she was mad), and had hidden my body somewhere in her big house. It had been searched quite thoroughly, in fact, by the county sheriff and a half-dozen of his men. They had found an unrecognizable mass of bones and gray flesh—all that was left of poor Luke—and that discovery served to deepen the suspicion that my body, too, was indeed hidden somewhere in the house.

"Let me in, Lemuel," I said through the window.

He didn't hear me. Since my transformation, I had slowly been losing control of my ability to speak, because, very simply, I had lost my ability to *hear*, in the normal sense of the word. So my speech patterns had steadily disintegrated until, that night, at Lemuel's window, what he heard from me were polysyllabic grunting sounds. He shrieked again and I heard myself say, "Oh hell, Lemuel, open the damned window, I want to talk to you!"

Then, through him, I heard what he was hearing, and realized that I was scaring the hell out of him. And because I could not enter his bedroom unless invited, I went away, into a stand of piney woods just behind his house, sat down at the base of a tree, with my legs straight, my hands folded on my lap, my head back, and I tried to sort things out.

Lemuel appeared an hour later.

"Jesus, Gawd, Elmo," he said, awestruck, "we thought you was dead for sure." He stood over me with his hands thrust into his pockets, and his torso bent slightly forward, as if to see me better in the darkness. He had put on a pair of blue jeans and a buttonless, threadbare green shirt. His huge square head bobbed slightly as he talked, as an infant's will. "We thought Regina Watson had done you in—we thought you was dead for sure, Elmo."

"I am," I said, and of course he did not understand me; he had heard only a kind of extended, low-pitched belch.

"I cain't understand you, Elmo, I cain't understand you," he said, and it clearly upset him.

So there, with him, in those piney woods, I learned to speak solely by listening to myself through others.

I said to him again, "I am," heard, through his ears, only a low-pitched belching sound.

"I cain't understand you, Elmo." He bent further

127

forward so his face was close to mine. "I cain't understand you, Elmo." He cupped his hand at his ear.

"I am!" I said again, very slowly. And as I heard myself through him I altered what I was saying, slightly. "I am!" I said again, repeated it once, then again, and again, until, at last, it began to sound less like a belch and more like speech. But it was still unintelligible.

Lemuel straightened, put his hand back into his pants pocket, began to weep.

I kicked him just below the knee; he liked it—someone was in authority and it wasn't him. I said once more, "I am!"

He grinned. "You am what, Elmo?" he said.

"I'm *dead*!"

His grin vanished. "You am 'dird', Elmo? What's 'dird'?" He was frantic with frustration.

"Dead!" I screamed.

He understood. He took a couple of steps backward. "You cain't be dead, Elmo," he said, his voice trembling. "How can you be dead and still be walking around, tappin' at my window, and sittin' there kickin' at me?!"

"You're an idiot!" I screamed at him.

"What, Elmo?" He was still backing away from me. He stopped. "What? You got to speak up, Elmo!"

"I need you," I told him.

"Need what?" He took a step forward, bent over again, his grin reappeared. "You need what, Elmo?"

"I need *you*!" I told him.

He understood. His grin broadened. He bent over

further so his mouth was near my ear and whispered to me, "Whatchoo need me for, Elmo? Whatchoo want me to do?"

"I'm hungry," I told him.

"Hawngry?!"

"Hungry!" I screamed at him.

"Hawngry? Whatchoo hawngry for, Elmo? I got some food back at the house I can bring ya. Whatchoo hawngry for?"

He was desperate to please me. "Blood!" I told him.

"Huh?" he said. "I dunno what that is, Elmo, tell me what that is."

I reached up and took a slice from his forearm with my nails, which had become very long and very sharp. He watched dumbly as the blood trickled out. I pointed. "That!" I bellowed.

He stuck his arm out to me. "Take some then, Elmo. What you want it for? Take some!"

I pushed him away.

"You know you feel awful, awful cold, Elmo."

"I'm dead, you idiot!"

He thought about this. It was always extremely difficult to read him. His thoughts seemed mired in molasses, and just as slow. He said, finally, "I guess maybe you are dead, Elmo. I'm awful sorry." Another grin. "Who kill'tcha?"

"Regina Watson," I answered.

He nodded earnestly. "I thought so, I thought so," he said. "Tha's jus' what I told ever-body, Elmo."

It was an hour later that we did our first murder together. We did it near Hanford, at the home of a

129

friend of my father's, a widower named Ray Wiggins who lived with his nineteen-year-old daughter and fourteen-year-old son in an old, tumble-down farmhouse. I was after any of them, it didn't matter which one, male or female, young or old, just as long as the blood flowed within them and I could get at it.

That's what Lemuel was for.

"You walk pretty good, Elmo," he said. We were a little less than a mile from Wiggins' house at the time and moving through a field of barley that Wiggins had planted; he'd allowed it to become overgrown with weeds. We were walking side by side, Lemuel with his hands in his pockets and his head lowered so he could avoid rocks and clods of dirt, although he stumbled quite often in the darkness, and I with my arms straight and my head erect. "I mean, you walk *real* good considerin' you're dead, Elmo."

"I never had trouble walking, Lemuel," I said.

To the north, toward Wiggins' house, Lemuel heard a dog begin to bark fitfully. He stopped walking. "Lord, Elmo," he said, "I don't wanna mess with no dog, why don't we forget it, huh, why don't we do this some other night, tomorrow night, we'll do it tomorrow night, Elmo—"

I slapped him. His huge body slipped to the right; he nearly fell. "Jees, Elmo, that *hurts*!" He rubbed his cheek. "Jees, that hurts. I wish you wouldn'ta done that—"

"Shut up, Lemuel." He shut up. He continued rubbing his cheek. To the north the dog's barking grew louder, more fitful, and Lemuel glanced toward the sound. I said, "Do you know what I want you to do, Lemuel?"

"Sure I do, Elmo."

"What do I want you to do?"

"You want I should bring one of the Wigginses out here to ya, isn't that right?"

"That's right, Lemuel."

"Why?"

"Because I'm hungry, dammit!"

"Uh-huh." He stopped rubbing his cheek and glanced toward the sound of the barking dog again. The barking was getting louder, the dog was getting closer. Lemuel said again, "Uh-huh," and added, "Why you hungry if you're dead, Elmo?"

"Idiot!"

"Tha's true enough, Elmo, but it does seem awful strange to me that a dead man would be hungry."

"Idiot!" I said again.

"Why don'tchoo eat that dog that's comin' here to eat *us*, Elmo, instead of eatin' one of the Wigginses, I mean, why don'tcha do that?"

I slapped him once more, harder. He fell.

I started for Wiggins' house. Moments later, Lemuel scrambled to his feet and was beside me again. "You know you're real strong, Elmo, how come you're so strong?" Before I could answer him he was talking about the dog again, which was very close now, and had begun to bray, as if it had picked up a scent. Lemuel said, "It's a fuckin' hound dog, Elmo, it's a fuckin' hound dog—"

"I'm not interested," I said.

"Well *I* sure am. Shit, Elmo—*I* sure am, 'cuz it's *me* he's gonna latch onto, you know that—"

The dog appeared just ahead of us. It was growling deep in its throat.

"Kill it!" I told Lemuel.

"I cain't *kill* it," he said.

"Of course you can. Go and kill it!"

The dog lunged. My right hand shot out, found its throat, and in moments the dog was dead.

"Sheee-it!" Lemuel breathed.

"Next time—" I began.

"Sheee-it, Elmo," he cut in. "How'd you do that, how'd you do that?" He started to laugh. "Where'd you learn somethin' like that, where'd you learn to do that?" His laugh grew louder and quicker. I realized that he was losing himself, that the reality of the events of the past few hours was finally sinking in. So I slapped him again. He fell; I leaned over him: "*Next* time, Lemuel," I began and pointed stiffly at him, "*you're* going to be the one to do it, not *me*, do you understand?"

He was on his side, hand to his jaw. "Sure I understand, Elmo. Sure I do. Doesn't make no difference to me."

"Good." I extended my hand. "Get up, now, the morning's coming." He took my hand, recoiled— "Jees, you're colder than a witch's tit, Elmo!"—took my hand again, got to his feet, and we started again for Wiggins' house, which was visible only as a low, black silhouette on the horizon.

We stopped close enough to the house that we could see someone walking about inside, back and forth in front of that one light, and Lemuel whispered, "Why don'tchoo go on in there yerself, Elmo? Why do I have to do it?"

"I've told you why," I answered.

"No, you ain't. You ain't told me doodly squat, 'cept I gotta do this and I gotta do that."

"Weren't you my friend, Lemuel? Weren't you my best friend?"

"I still am, Elmo. It don't matter to me that yer dead, I don't care that yer dead, why should I care? All I wanta know is why *I* gotta go on in there?"

"Because you can and I can't. It's as simple as that. If they don't let me in, I can't go in. And I'm damned hungry, Lemuel. I don't have time to mess around, so if you *don't* go in there"—I grabbed him by the shirt collar—"if you *don't* go in there I'll tear you apart!"

I let him go. He backed away a few steps, his mouth fell open, he stared wide-eyed at me for quite a while, said, at last, "You would, wouldn'tcha?" then turned and went to the house while I watched.

He knocked once, softly. Nothing. He knocked again, and again. He glanced in my direction, shrugged, knocked again. Moments later the door opened. A woman appeared—Wiggins' daughter. She was dressed in a white nightgown that she was holding up with her right hand so it wouldn't drag on the floor. I heard her say, impatiently, "Whatchoo want, boy? You know it's the middle of the night." Lemuel nodded. Then, for the very first time since I'd known him he took me completely by surprise. He said, "I do, ma'am," and grabbed her around the waist,

133

threw her over his shoulder and jogged back to me. He was laughing all the while, she was screaming and cursing, and inside Wiggins' house several more lights came on.

When he got to me—I was standing just inside the perimeter of the barley field—he said through his laughter, "Here ya go, Elmo!" and threw her to the ground so she landed on her back. She took several quick, shallow breaths, the wind knocked out of her, then lapsed into unconsciousness. I bent over her at once and began to satisfy myself.

Ray Wiggins appeared at the front door of his house seconds later. "Marietta!" he called frantically. "Marietta!" I heard a shotgun being cocked, heard him take a step off his porch. His son appeared behind him in the doorway.

I looked up from Marietta very briefly and said to Lemuel, "Go and kill them. I cannot be disturbed here."

He nodded once, briskly, grinningly, and stepped out of the field, into the pale light from the house.

"She's over here, Mr Wiggins!" I heard him call, and it passed fleetingly across my mind that he was betraying me. Then I read amusement in him, and expectation. "Over here, right over here!" he said again. "She's done hurt herself, Mr Wiggins!"

"Jus' you stay right still, boy!" Wiggins commanded.

"Right still!" Wiggins' son echoed.

"You know me, Mr Wiggins," Lemuel called, "I'm Lemuel Palminteer from off Phillips Road—you know me!"

Wiggins' son, Earl, said, "I know him, Pa."

134

Ray Wiggins said, his voice growing louder as he spoke because he was drawing closer, "Yeah, I know him, too." Then he called, "Marietta! Marietta!"—closer—"You answer me, now! Earl, do you see her?"

Lemuel said, "She's right in there, Mr Wiggins, right in there. She's hurt herself, come take a look—"

"Go and look, Earl!" Wiggins told his son.

"Yeah, come on over here quick, Earl!" Lemuel said, and a tiny laugh escaped him that neither Earl nor Ray Wiggins could have heard.

"Yeah, Pa," Earl Wiggins said, and I heard him move through the tall grass at a fast walk.

"Right in here, Earl!" Lemuel said.

"Jus' stay right where you are, Lemuel!" commanded Ray Wiggins.

Then I felt someone staring down at me as I fed on Marietta Wiggins. I stopped briefly, looked up, saw Earl, saw his mouth move silently, saw a big arm go around his throat, saw his whole body being turned, heard Ray Wiggins let loose with his shotgun, heard Earl scream, "Pa, don't shoot me!" but I could feel his sudden and immense pain, I could feel him die, and I heard Lemuel begin to laugh again. Ray Wiggins let loose with the other barrel of the shotgun, and I heard Earl Wiggins' body being dropped.

"Where ya stayin' at?" Lemuel asked me an hour later. In the east the sky was beginning to lighten. We were on Phillips Road, nearing Regina Watson's house.

"Any place that it's dark," I said.

135

"Why's that?"

"Because I need the dark."

"Uh-huh." He fell silent for several moments, then went on, "I liked doin' that, Elmo. I liked killin' those people. It felt good. We gonna be doin' it again?"

I said nothing.

"Elmo, we gonna do that again?" Lemuel repeated.

"Get away from me!" I hissed at him.

"Huh? Whatchoo mean?"

"Get the hell away from me! Jesus, get the hell away from me!"

"Sure, Elmo," he said quiveringly, and ran.

I spent that day in the cellar of an abandoned farmhouse not far from my own house on Phillips Road.

But that evening, the hunger caught up with me again, and I sought Lemuel out. For several years, he'd been living by himself in his parents' house, ever since they'd gone north without him.

He had Marietta Wiggins in the house. He'd propped her up in a big, over-stuffed, battered blue chair in the kitchen, and when I appeared he nodded enthusiastically at her. "She ain't dead, Elmo. She ain't dead! She is almost, but not quite."

But when I bent over her, I found that he was wrong.

11

———

I know so well about compulsion.

Here, deep, deep inside this creature, that's where I am. Mrs Land's baby boy, brought into the world at home on a bright April day in 1907, pink as a spring sunrise, plopped into a basinette, thanks given, a new life for the world.

Here I am, inside this creature, inside this corpse that can still walk about. Here. Behind the medulla oblongata, on my knees, hiding.

And I do the things that I have to do because the monstrous need ends then. Peace comes. The infant sleeps. Small squeaking noises drift up from it.

I can't help what I do.

We all have our crosses to bear.

So I tore little Georgie apart and I threw him down and I heard his skull go *Sploosh!* into a rock. I didn't look, I still knew something about beauty and I knew that I had made him into something very ugly.

I can't help it, I can't help it—I'm like a termite eating someone's house up. I can't be reasoned with,

I can only be exterminated, and that is so terribly difficult.

Impossible, really, it's so difficult.

Even God doesn't want to do it.

But of course, no one can reason with Him, either.

And so, to sleep.

Friday

Jeff asked, "Do you think there's anyone else still alive?" He wanted me to say no. He wants desperately to believe that he's the last human.

"Yes," I said. His face sagged. "Somewhere."

"I don't think so," he said. He sounded sullen, as if he were on the verge of a pout. "I think we're what's left of the human race, Elmo. I'm sure of it."

He came to the house after sunset. He had a big, gray wool coat on, explained that it was pretty cold for so late in the year, and asked if he could come in. I took him into the library (Tad Hamilton likes very much to read; she has thousands of books), and sat him down on a yellow loveseat.

He went on, gesturing expansively and grimly, for show, "I don't think there's anyone left but you and me, Elmo."

I said nothing. I was seated near him on a wooden high-backed chair, with my legs crossed.

He went on, "Actually, I came to this village looking for a woman." He let a small devilish smirk play across his lips. "I didn't find her. I went to her house, but I didn't find her. I found her mother and her father. They were dead."

138

"Did you burn the house?" I asked.

He looked startled; he wasn't. He said, after a moment, "I plan to. Tomorrow, I think. But they're all there, all the people from the village—everyone I could find, anyway. They're piled up in the living room, and in the kitchen, and in the bedrooms." He grimaced. "It's a hell of a house to walk into—"

"I can imagine," I said.

He nodded again. "Yes, tomorrow for sure. I've got to do it right. If I can find enough gasoline I can do it right. The house is made of stone, you know—it'll make a great incinerator." I could feel that he was drifting off. He glanced away, at a shelf loaded with books. "Is this your house, Elmo?"

"I'm using it," I said.

"Lots of books, huh? I used to be a literary agent. Did I tell you that? So I know about books."

"Yes. You told me."

"Lots of books." A brief pause. "What were you, Elmo?"

"A pharmacist."

"Oh. Yes. We need pharmacists." He realized that he was drifting and it bothered him. "I don't know for what," he went on. He shook his head. "I'm sorry. That was a stupid thing to say."

"But now, I just relax," I told him. It put him at ease. I went on, "What was her name?"

He answered at once, "'Lizbeth. Elizabeth, really, but she thought 'Lizbeth had class. Maybe it does."

"She had enormous boobs, huh?" I said, because it was a phrase that was lingering about in his head.

He tried to look surprised, but another devilish

smirk appeared on his lips and stayed there as he spoke. "Yes. She was quite a woman, Elmo." The smirk broadened. He was remembering his last time with her, at her parents' house. He and 'Lizbeth were upstairs, her parents downstairs; he and 'Lizbeth had gone upstairs, ostensibly to paint a spare bedroom. "A very acrobatic woman, Elmo," he continued. "Young and acrobatic."

"We remember only the good times," I said.

"Maybe," he said, clearly unconvinced. "We remember the bad times, too. Very clearly." He paused, though not long enough for me to speak. He hurried on, "I didn't realize, Elmo, how much people meant to me until the war ended." He looked away, looked back, continued, "It was probably—what?—half a day after the war started. Not even half a day. A couple of hours. And I was trying to clear out of my house—I had a small house, Elmo—I was trying to get all the stuff that means something to a man, my stereo, you know, my stereo and my bowling trophies, because they told us over the radio to get out, to go to the country, and that's what I was going to do. And I was loading this stuff into my Camaro—I had a twenty-year-old Camaro, Elmo, and it was *mint*—and while I was putting my stuff in it I saw my neighbor across the street pull up. His name was John Francis, Elmo, and he was a *jerk*! With a capital J. I remember once my dog, Hobo, went over to his front yard and this guy comes runnin' out with a gun and he threatens to blow Hobo's head off. And another time I was having a party at my place. It wasn't late. It was maybe ten, or eleven, and the party wasn't *that* loud.

140

But old John Francis calls the cops. Jesus! Anyway, he pulls up, this *jerk* pulls up while I'm loading my Camaro and he gets out of his car and I look and I see that he's got this *stuff* all over him, and that he's shaking, and I call to him, 'Hey, John, what you got all over ya?' Well, you know what he had all over him, don'tcha? Fall-out. And it was killing him right then and there it was so strong. Well, Jesus, Elmo, he turned around and held his hands out as if he was going to hug me, and he called, 'Help me, for Christ's sake, help me!' And I did what I could. I hosed him down. I told him to strip, and he did, and I hosed him down, and I kept saying, 'Jesus, I'm sorry, I'm sorry,' as if the fact that he was going to die was *my* fault." Jeff shrugged. "Because, I don't know, he was a jerk, sure, but he was still my neighbor, he was another human being, and no way did he deserve to get that crap all over him."

Saturday

I found a small boy hiding out back of a double-wide mobile home in one of those aluminum sheds that people store gardening tools and lawn-mowers in. He was a skinny boy and incoherent and he had miserable, hard-edged memories running about inside him. I took my fill from him, found some canned food, forced it into his mouth, and he was thankful. I brought him blankets, too.

He calls me *Daddy*.

12

___

Monday

A group of six men and three women who call themselves "survivalists" has come here. They say they've been in the woods for the last year, since the war ended, that they've been living underground to escape the radiation, and have been surviving on a diet of dried fruits and vegetables, canned foods and, recently, an occasional freshly killed animal.

But all of them are dying, because the animals they've eaten were loaded with radiation, even though they waited several months before hunting.

And all of them exude self-confidence. Each is wonderfully certain that they, and their kind, will "carry on for the human race".

They are former city dwellers. Two of the men were CPAs, one was an advertising account executive, one an attorney, one of the women was a tax lawyer, the other was an executive secretary for a toothbrush manufacturer.

They all have children back there in the woods; their children are dying, too.

And, like Jeff, these people see their situation as grimly romantic. Maybe they're right. I don't know, I have no opinion. What am I? I'm a leach, a parasite. I stopped needing to have opinions eighty years ago.

Wednesday

One of the survivalists came to the house tonight and said he needed a favor. His name is Mike and he's big, ruddy-complexioned, very healthy-looking, despite the radiation that's gobbling him up.

I said to him, "What kind of favor?"

"Can we talk about it inside, please?" he answered, and I showed him into the library and sat him down in the same seat that Jeff uses. I explained that I'd just run out of provisions, even coffee, sorry, and then he got to the point.

He's dark-haired, square-jawed, a tad more muscular than he should be, and he has a quick, disarming smile.

"I need a friend, Mr Land," he said.

"A friend?" I said. "I don't understand."

His quick smile appeared. He fidgeted slightly. "I haven't had a friend since the war started." He nodded obliquely to his left. "They're all straight."

"Straight?"

"Hetero."

"Oh," I said, and I sat in a chair that was close to him, put my hands behind my head, tried to look casual. "Oh," I said again and attempted a smile. His smile broadened. "You mean 'hetero*sexual*', don't you?" I said.

143

He looked uncomfortable. "Are you playing games with me, Mr Land?"

"Yes," I answered at once, "I am. Can I tell you why?"

"Yes, I wish that you would."

I unclasped my hands from behind my head, leaned forward, beckoned him to lean forward too—he did—and I whispered to him in a tone that was dripping with melodrama. "I'm a vampire, Mike," and I attempted a smile again, nodded once, saw that he was smiling too, went on, "And *I* haven't had a friend for eight decades."

I leaned back. He was still leaning forward, still smiling. He had his big reddish hands together, elbows on his knees, and he said, "Can I assume, then, that your answer is no, Mr Land?" He sounded hurt. Clearly, he hadn't believed a word I'd told him.

I said to him, "And I'll tell you another thing, Mike; you're not going to leave this house tonight."

His smile quivered. "I'm not?" he said.

"That's right. I'm sorry."

He sat back in his chair and tried desperately hard to look unconcerned. He glanced quickly about. "You do a lot of reading, don't you, Mr Land?"

"No," I said.

I heard in his brain, *Jesus, he really thinks he's a damned vampire*? And I said, "Of course I believe I'm a vampire, Mike. I have no choice but to believe it, just as you have no choice but to believe that you have ten fingers and ten toes." Then I stood and gave him a very large grin.

I have marvellous vampire canines. Most of the

144

Join the Leisure Horror Book Club and
GET 2 FREE BOOKS NOW—
An $11.98 value!

┌─ Yes! I want to subscribe to ─
the Leisure Horror Book Club.

Please send me my **2 FREE BOOKS**. I have enclosed $2.00 for shipping/handling. Each month I'll receive the two newest Leisure Horror selections to preview for 10 days. If I decide to keep them, I will pay the Special Members Only discounted price of just $4.25 each, a total of $8.50, plus $2.00 shipping/handling. This is a **SAVINGS OF AT LEAST $3.48** off the bookstore price. There is no minimum number of books I must buy and I may cancel the program at any time. In any case, the **2 FREE BOOKS** are mine to keep.

─── *Not available in Canada.* ───

NAME: _____

ADDRESS: _____

CITY: _____ **STATE:** _____

COUNTRY: _____ **ZIP:** _____

TELEPHONE: _____

E-MAIL: _____

SIGNATURE: _____

older members of my species have allowed theirs to rot and chip, but a vampire without good canines is like a cat without a tongue—if it can't eat, it won't survive.

Mike thought my canines were marvellous, too. "Those are very impressive, Mr Land," he said, and a fleeting image of me winning them at a carnival sideshow passed through his head.

I took a step toward him. He stayed put. He figured that he had a good fifty pounds on me, and most of that was in muscle. He said, his voice quivering slightly, "When did you become a vampire, Mr Land?"

I answered, "Long before you were born, Mike."

"That's impressive, too, Mr Land. You don't look much past forty. What's your secret—abstinence, hard work?"

I took another step toward him. He began to squirm. "I don't want to have to hurt you, Mr Land," he said.

"Please call me Elmo," I said.

"You're from the south?"

"I'm from you," I said.

I was above him now, and my canines were fully bared. He brought his knee up hard into my groin. I felt the same kind of slight, tickling sensation that I felt when Jeff's coffee had filtered through me.

"Christ!" Mike whispered.

"I do like that," I said, and bent over him. He scooted out from beneath me—taking me by surprise—and ran to the far corner of the room, between the window and door. "I don't want to hurt you, Elmo," he said again. "But if I have to, I will."

"I wish that you could, Mike," I said.

He resides now in the cellar, as poor Luke did in Regina Watson's house, and I haven't decided what I'll do with him. It occurs to me that we're both members of oppressed minorities. He's gay. I'm a vampire. So the chances are that as a gesture of good-will—a member of one oppressed minority lends a hand to a member of another—I'll let him go. It depends on my hunger, of course. *Everything* depends on my hunger.

And so, to sleep.

Thursday

The others, all eight of them, came looking for Mike very early this morning. I chose not to answer the door. I chose to stay well within the bowels of the house, where the knife-edged memories of the woman named Tad Hamilton are strong and exciting.

"Come in, please!" I called to them. And they did.

An older woman with a high forehead and intelligent, gray eyes was in the lead. She said, "Are you ill, Mr Land?"

I was seated in a big, high-backed chair that was facing a corner of the room where the light was weakest. Through their eyes I saw what they were seeing—my hands on the arms of the chair, the back of my head.

"No," I answered. "I feel very good. Are you looking for your friend?"

"Yes," she said. "We have reason to believe that he came here last night."

"He did," I said, which surprised her.

She asked, "And when did he leave?"

I answered at once, "He didn't. He's still here." I allowed a brief and meaningful pause, then I added, "And so are you." I got a minute's worth of stunned silence. Then the woman said, "We don't understand that. Of course we're here, and if Mr Trumbull is here, too, as you've said—"

"He is," I cut in, and said again, "And *so* are *you*."

"Why does that sound like a threat, Mr Land?"

"Because that's what it is, Mrs Jarvis," I said.

There was nervous fidgeting in the room. I heard a rifle being cocked.

"How do you know my name?" the woman asked.

"You told me," I answered.

"No I didn't."

I heard another weapon being cocked, a handgun.

"That's correct," I said.

More nervous fidgeting. I could feel that one of the men was about to be violently ill.

The woman named Jarvis took a deep breath, as if to give herself courage. "Please tell us where Mr Trumbull is. We don't want any trouble here."

I answered, "He's in this house. I'm afraid he's had a very troubled night."

"You're playing games with us, Mr Land."

I shook my head. "That's just what Mr Trumbull said, Mrs Jarvis."

I felt them glance confusedly at each other. Another weapon was cocked, a shotgun. The man with the handgun—the man who was about to be ill—levelled it at the back of my head. I could feel the tension in him, his knees were beginning to knock, and I knew

147

that in only a few seconds his finger would tighten on the trigger. I had no idea, nor did I care, if his bullet would miss me—he had never before carried a gun, they had always frightened him, but the war had given him a kind of tense courage.

I said to him, "You be very careful with that thing or you'll embarrass us all." I felt sudden and unreasoning anger push through him.

He fired.

"Good Christ!" someone breathed.

One of the men wrestled the gun from the man who'd fired and threw him to the floor. He lay face down and mumbled sincere apologies into the rug.

I stood, canines bared. The man with the shotgun fired, the man with the rifle fired, I felt a slight itching sensation where the slugs hit me—in the chest, my left arm, just above my forehead, along the hairline.

The man on the floor continued mumbling apologies into the rug, clearly oblivious to what was happening above him. Mrs Jarvis kicked at him; "Get up you idiot, get up!"

"Why don't you leave him here?" I suggested.

She kicked him again, "Get the hell *up*, Josephson!"

The man with the rifle fired once more. He was a hunter, usually very good with his weapon, but a sudden case of nerves was upon him and the bullet merely grazed my right hand and tore into the wallpaper behind me. I glanced around at it, then back at the hunter. I attempted a smile. "That's not friendly," I said.

And by this time the man with the shotgun had

reloaded and was ready to fire again. The air in the room was blue with panic.

Jarvis commanded, "Don't waste it, Bill, don't waste it!" meaning the shotgun shells, and he nodded quickly and lowered his weapon.

"You're an intelligent woman, Mrs Jarvis," I said. They were backing away from me, now

"What *are* you?" she screeched. "What in the fuck *are* you?"

I answered simply enough, "I am you." They turned and fled, leaving poor Josephson behind. He was still mumbling apologies into the rug.

Jeff came over late in the evening, after I'd had time to find other clothes—a red plaid shirt, blue jeans, tan Wallabees—and had also applied liberal amounts of some pancake make-up I'd found in Tad Hamilton's bedroom.

He said that the survivalists had gone away, that he was thankful for it because they had made him nervous, and I told him I thought they'd be back.

"Anyway," he said, "I have a gun, and I'll be ready for them. You've got to protect what's yours, right, Elmo?"

"And what *is* yours, Jeff?" I asked.

"This whole village, of course. I control it, so it's mine." A short pause; then, "How you feeling, Elmo? Are you okay? You look ill."

"It's the arthritis."

"Oh. Yes. Sorry." He nodded at me. "I'll protect you, too," he said.

"I don't need it. Thanks."

"Sure you do. I'm younger, I'm stronger, and I've got the gun, so *I'll* protect *you*. I'm really happy to do it, Elmo. I like you. And besides, a man's got to have something to protect."

"I don't need it," I said again, with emphasis on the word *need*. "I really don't *need* it. I'm stronger than you think—"

He cut in, "Do you know that you're getting smaller, Elmo?"

"No I'm not."

"Sure you are. Maybe it's just the way you're sitting, but I'd swear that you're shorter than you were last week." He grinned. I read amusement in him, and it annoyed me. "And you're beginning to slur your words—"

"My speech is perfect," I interrupted, my pride wounded.

"Sorry?"

"I said that my speech is perfect."

"Nothing's 'perfect', Elmo." He stood, smiled down at me. "Thanks for a stimulating talk, Elmo. Get some rest, okay." Then he turned and left the house.

I heard something today as I slept. I heard someone singing, a woman singing, as if she were calling to me from a great distance. It was an extraordinarily beautiful sound, and it stopped almost at once, as if someone had closed a heavy door between us to keep us apart.

13

I saw Regina Watson once after my transformation. It was early Christmas morning, 1928, and for the first time in almost half a century snow had come to Hanford, Kentucky. Not much, two inches perhaps, and doubtless it was gone by midday. But to my eyes, even then—a year after my transformation—it was very pleasant. I remember standing near the house on Phillips Road, just inside a stand of piney woods, and watching it collect on rooftops and chimneys and on my father's Buick. I had never, in life, seen anything like that snow. Even in the darkness it glistened. It floated through the still air and onto the landscape with exquisite grace, as if each flake were caught up in its own beauty and was sharing itself with the world.

And as I watched, I felt another presence in those piney woods, something as graceful as the snow. Something, I knew, that was moving inexorably toward me through the dark.

I did not know it was Regina Watson.

I thought it was some night creature prowling out of hunger and confused by the snow.

Then I felt my father get out of his bed, because of the cold, and go to a window, and look out. Through his eyes I saw the wide, graceful flakes piling up everywhere, moving in the darkness like moths, not quite getting all the way down into the piney woods, turning the tree-tops white. "Myrna," he called, "come see this here." But she was asleep.

I felt him smile. I felt his pleasure at the snow. I saw his eyes linger on me for several seconds. "Myrna," he called again, "come here." But she stayed asleep. He continued to watch the snow collect, and as he watched, he said to himself that he didn't remember that stump being there, at the front of the piney woods, because he didn't know, of course, that the stump was his son. His son was buried somewhere in Regina Watson's house. God knew where. He'd been through it a dozen times, he had torn the house apart, in fact.

Then his gaze settled on other things—on his Buick, on his own reflection from the window, on the snow again, on me. He saw Regina Watson come up behind me through the woods. He saw her put her arms around me.

Then he looked at the snow again and he thought it was beautiful. He hoped it would last through Christmas Day.

14

Hiram and Betty, Vampire Hunters, first encountered me just outside Charleston in 1929, in a small farming community called Bridgeston.

Hiram's surname was Shepard, Betty's was Singer— Hiram Shepard and Betty Singer—and I believe that I actually miss them, they were good company (and I was *always* in their company while they were after me). Their tensions, their fears, their anxieties were like music to me, as if the background of my existence were filled with something vibrant and real (because *they* were), something Mrs Land's baby boy could grab hold of and with it make himself human again.

I was staying in the house of a man named Davies in Bridgeston. He was very old, and he fancied that he was very wise (and in his way he was), and he thought it was "providential" that he should play host to a "poor damned creature" like myself. He provided me with a pitch-dark cellar room, a coffin made of pine, which he fashioned himself—I have since learned, quite by accident, that coffins are affectations, so I've not used one for decades—and a promise that "God made you, so God will protect you, with my help."

In those days there were lingering traces of affection in me, like the remnants of a dream, and I believe that I actually felt affection for him.

He was a bachelor who drank sparingly, had a woman over now and again, and spent most of his free time tending to his house, which would have fallen down around him otherwise. I'd been staying with him a month when Hiram Shepard and Betty Singer came to the village.

Memories move around inside my head like snowflakes. It is so cold, so cold here. All of these are memories. I live a thousand years ahead of the world.

Sunday, again

In the village I can feel that the dead are finally moving off. Something is calling to them—I have no idea what, because it hasn't called to me. I know it's calling only to them because they tell me it is—"I hear singing!" they say—but I can't hear a thing.

They're happy the pain is over. They had imagined an eternity of pain, such as I have.

The man named Davies woke me at around noon. "Elmo," he whispered, "some people are looking for you." He was agitated. "Come with me." He took a few steps back from the pine coffin. I sat up in it, heard a cacophony of minds around me, in the village, and reflexively I put my hands to my ears and groaned, as if in pain.

Davies said again, "Elmo, come with me, please."

"Damn you!" I hissed.

"Elmo, you must hurry."

I took my hands from my ears, lay down again, saw Davies rush to the coffin, saw him put his hands on my arms. "Elmo!" he cried, and I literally threw him across the room. He hit the far wall, glanced off it, landed face down on the dirt floor. "Let me sleep!" I commanded. "Let me sleep!" And a few minutes later he pushed himself to his feet and went back upstairs. He had already forgiven me. He thought that he understood me, which was a source of pride for him, so he had no choice but to forgive me.

Then, from above, I heard Hiram Shepard and Betty Singer knock at his door. He opened it at once. "Yes," he said, his voice heavy with pretended impatience, "what do you want?"

Betty offered him her hand. He took it clumsily. She told him her name, briskly introduced Hiram, and went on, "We're looking for a man who believes that he's a vampire."

"I'm the only man here," Davies protested.

Betty said, "Then you know what a vampire is?"

"No," Davies answered. "No," he repeated, "tell me what it is." But his voice was strident, his tone false, and Hiram and Betty realized at once that he was lying. Hiram stepped forward. "If you're hiding him,

155

sir, then we must warn you that he's killed a dozen people, already—"

"I'm the only man here," Davies said again.

"May we look in your house?" Betty asked.

"No. I'm the only man here, there's no one else here. Now get out!" He slammed the door.

Later that evening, an hour after dusk, I left Davies' house by the rear door and made my way toward a farm just outside Bridgeston. Some people were smelt fishing there, in a creek that wound through Bridgeston and eventually found its way to the Black River. They would be easy targets out in the open, in the darkness—I had, in fact, made victims of smelt fishermen in several other rural communities throughout Kentucky.

I was carrying a net, and a kerosene lantern. I was wearing a fisherman's hat, a dark, spring jacket and hip boots—all paraphernalia that Davies had provided because I'd told him that "in life one of my passions was smelt fishing", so he pitied me. (He didn't believe for a moment that I was what I claimed to be.)

I saw a long line of kerosene lanterns and lit faces at the creek, at least fifty men dipping their nets in and pulling smelt out. And as I made my own way along the creek bank—nodding when one of them said hi, or, occasionally, when one of them called me by someone else's name ("Hi, Daniel," one said, because faces tend to look similar in the light from kerosene lamps)—I was searching for one who was not within easy earshot of the others, maybe someone who was looking for a particularly good spot to fish that he was going to keep all to himself.

I found one such man around a bend in the creek, where it had formed a shallow pool that smelt spawning tended to get caught in. It wouldn't be long, of course, before some of the others found the same pool, so I started my business at once. When I was a couple of yards away from the man I said hello. I held my lantern far away from me, at an oblique angle so it cast harsh shadows across my face and made me difficult to recognize (and so increased the chances that I would be mistaken for someone else).

"Hi," the man fishing said, and I saw him reach into his back pocket and pull something out.

"The fishing's pretty good here?" I said.

"The fishing here is terrific, my friend." His lantern was on the creek bank behind him, and it was flickering slightly, as if running out of fuel.

"Mind if I join you?"

"Sure," he answered, "there's enough here for both of us."

"Thanks," I said, and made my way along the bank toward him. "My name's Daniel," I went on. "What's yours?"

"My name is Hiram," he said, then with wonderful quickness turned his torso around in the waist-deep water and with a kind of sliding, underhand motion tossed the contents of the thing he'd had in his back pocket at me. I was bathed in it, it burned abominably, and for one very quick moment I remembered a time, several years before, that my mother had been making candy and some boiling sugar had splattered across my chest.

I dropped the lantern. I believe that I screamed. I ran.

Lemuel was not with me there, in Bridgeston. He was in a North Carolina prison, awaiting execution.

We do not dream. We can't. This thing called a brain inside our heads is nothing more than a liquified mass of dead tissue. No current passes through it. It might as well be water (and in some of us who are very old, that's precisely what it is). In sleep we are freed, we become a part of existence—we have no hunger, or memory, or need. We *become* all that *is*. We experience nothing. We experience all. We are the sow bug underfoot, the stalk of wheat falling to the farmer's blade, the infant routing at its mother's breast, the stack of cumulus that some small boy makes monsters of, a summer leaf, the nose of a poet, mother of pearl.

It's not pleasant or unpleasant. We come back. We are forced back. We have pain. A million minds scream at us.

All that has changed since the war, of course. Instead of millions of minds there are now only a few, and they can do no more than whisper.

Jeff is whispering now. It's a whisper of pleasure because he's going to burn 'Lizbeth's house, at last. He has the gasoline, and the thought comes to him that he never liked 'Lizbeth's mother very much, anyway, which is a thought he finds distasteful, so he chases it off.

And there's another thought: *Elmo is a dead man*. It comes from deep inside him, from his instincts, and he doesn't believe it. He chases it off, too, and thinks again that he didn't like 'Lizbeth's mother very much. He lets the thought linger because it gives him more comfort now.

It's night here in Mumford and the fireflies are everywhere.

15

Monday

Do you believe in me? Hiram Shepard and Betty
Singer did. Holly did. Little George did, at last. But a
lot of others didn't, and they were entitled to their
disbelief, of course. It never mattered much to me. I
exist. I will always exist.

Tuesday Evening

Jeff said, "Want to know where I was, Elmo, when
the war started? I was at the dentist's office."

He was in the library, in his usual chair. I'd made a
cup of cocoa for him, and he was sipping it.

"Yes?" I said. I was seated near him. I was trying
hard to look relaxed, though that's very difficult with
a drastically deadened sense of touch.

He nodded grimly. "I was getting a route canal—I
hate route canals, have you ever had one?"

"Never."

"But it was a lady dentist—you don't see many lady
dentists, do you?—and that made it a little more

bearable." He grinned. "She had her radio on—elevator music, you know, background music—and she was in the middle of giving me like my twelfth shot of novocaine. I'm very sensitive to pain, Elmo."

"I'll keep that in mind."

"Thanks. And the announcer came on, the DJ, and he said something like, 'Well, folks, it's happened at last,' and from his tone I thought he was going to tell us something stupid, something frivolous, you know, like 'At last they've built a McDonald's on Wall Street,' something like that, so I listened and I didn't hear a thing from him for what must have been at least a minute or two, and then he came back on the air and said that we were to turn to our Conelrad stations— he said 'Con-L-rad,' I remember—and he said his station was going off the air. So I looked at the lady dentist and she was asking me if I was numb yet. I said to her, 'Didn't you hear that?' And she said, 'Hear what?' and I told her what and she shrugged and said, 'It's a test.'" He grinned again, but it was flat, and melancholy, then he went on, "But it wasn't a test, of course." He looked intently at me for several moments. "What'd you do to your head, Elmo?" he asked. I touched my head, started to answer, and he cut in, "No, your forehead. There." He pointed at the spot near my hairline where the survivalist's bullet had gone in.

"Oh," I said, and touched the spot. I studied my finger, saw a little pancake make-up on it, tried to see myself through Jeff's eyes. He was blocking me—not consciously, of course, it was his confusion that was blocking me (it's difficult to read through confusion) and I said that I had hit my head on something sharp. He didn't believe me. He said he hoped it didn't hurt much, glanced at his watch—which stopped working six months ago; he wears it out of habit—explained he had to get back to his house, "I listen for radio broadcasts about this time," he said, and he left.

I miss Lemuel. I'm not afraid to say that. I miss Lemuel nearly as much as I miss Lewis Perdue (though for wildly different reasons). Just as Jeff misses his dog. Lemuel was like a dog—he was obedient, strong, protective, loyal. It was his loyalty, in fact, that put him in that North Carolina prison and on death row.

We'd been together six months, moving about through Kentucky, Alabama, and Georgia, and we'd done a lot of walking. I didn't mind it; why would I mind it? But Lemuel started to complain that he was getting bunions and flat feet, and didn't I think it was time we got hold of a car?

We were close to the northern border of South Carolina, near the village of Champion. It was just past midnight, and I was homing in on a young, extremely vulnerable and willing woman asleep in a small house at the edge of the village, when Lemuel made his suggestion that we get a car. I was hungry. I'd gone without for several nights—after the first night of hunger, I tend to lose count—and so I was particularly out of sorts.

"That's a stupid suggestion," I told him.

He grinned his big, wide-open grin. "Yeah, it is,

ain't it, Elmo," he said. "What in hell we want with a car, anyway?"

We were about a mile from Champion, on a narrow, twisting, gravel road. It was mid-summer—Lemuel had told me more than once that it was "Unbearable hot, Elmo," which didn't bother me, of course—and a hundred feet or so ahead of us, where the road curved sharply to the right, we could see that the pitch darkness gave way to a wide, diffused spray of yellow light. "Hey," Lemuel said, nodding, "what's that up there, you think?" He'd gotten used to getting what was, for lack of a better word, telepathic information from me ("Hey, Elmo, which one of them girls there you think I can have just for the askin', huh?" or "Hey, Elmo, you think they's anybody around 'cuz I gotta piss here?" or "Hey, Elmo, be a warm day you think?" which was the kind of question I've always found difficult to answer, the *Be clairvoyant, Elmo* kind of question), and I answered him, "It's a gas station, Lemuel."

"A *gas* station, out here? What in hell for, Elmo?"

"To sell gas, of course!" I hissed.

"Good reason, Elmo," he said, grinning yet again.

I stopped walking suddenly, and stuck my hand out so Lemuel would stop too.

"Somepin wrong, Elmo?"

"There's a car coming," I said, and I yanked him to the side of the road where the brush was thick and would provide good cover. Moments later, we saw the headlights of a car appear to the left, from where we'd just come.

"It's jus' a car, Elmo," Lemuel said, and as he said

it, one of the car's tires blew out. I heard someone in the car curse, felt him stiff-leg the brake pedal. The car came to a halt a dozen yards from where we were hiding.

Another of Lemuel's big, stupid grins appeared. *"There's* a car, Elmo!" he whispered, and burst from the bushes, onto the road. He fell immediately into the glare of the car's headlights.

The man in the car stuck his head out the driver's window: "Who the hell are *you*, boy?" he called.

Lemuel answered joyfully, "I'm gonna take your car, I want your car!" He moved forward, stiffly, because he was very excited, while the man watched, half amused, half annoyed.

I felt the man's hand tighten around something cold. "You ain't gonna take *nothin'*, boy!" he called.

"Lemuel, you idiot, come back here, the man has a gun!" I said, but he didn't hear me, and I knew that it was time for me to act. I took one step onto the road. I stopped. For the first time I realized that the man driving had a passenger. Another man. A priest. An aged priest, to be sure, a priest who probably wouldn't last out the year, the driver's great-uncle, as it turned out. But a priest none the less. Someone who carried certain potent artifacts around with him. So I stepped back. The driver fired, hitting Lemuel in the right arm. Lemuel kept moving; he was enraged now. The man fired again, and hit Lemuel in the stomach. Lemuel was beside the car, now. He reached through the open window, took the man's throat in his good hand and crushed his larynx.

I felt the priest's old heart miss a few beats. The driver died. And Lemuel collapsed beside the car.

Cursing at many things—at Lemuel and his barbaric stupidity, at the man in the car, at the old priest, at my hunger, which ruled me—I moved off into the underbrush.

16

At last Jeff has burned 'Lizbeth's house. And though he'd never admit it, even to himself, he enjoyed the hell out of it, enjoyed watching the flames build, the house consumed. He even enjoyed the smell, though it made his stomach churn.

He's a very moral person, his conscience is well developed, it sits stiffly on him, like too much muscle, and he looks hunchbacked from it.

Poor man. He's got the whole world to play in now, but he doesn't know if it would be *right* to play the way he wants to.

And now he wonders, idly, just how interesting it would be to come and burn *this* house.

He said to me, "I feel *liberated*, Elmo, I feel so damned *liberated*." It was a little past sunset and he was standing just outside the door, a can of gasoline in one hand, a box of kitchen matches in the other.

"Are you planning to burn my house, Jeff?" I asked him.

He nodded solemnly. "Yes, Elmo. I'm sorry. You can go somewhere else, there are plenty of houses available, I didn't burn them all." He nodded to his left, toward the village. "There's a great big one over there, it's kind of a mansion, I guess—I think it would suit you." Something like amusement sped across his face.

I was standing in the doorway and was holding the screen door open with my left hand. I said, "I prefer this house, Jeff. I don't want to go somewhere else."

He protested, "But I'm going to *burn* it *down*, Elmo."

Again something like wry amusement passed across his face and for a moment I saw myself through his eyes. I saw that I was twitching nervously (a physical impossibility, of course), though I've always thought of myself as the very soul of composure and restraint. "You're tired, Jeff," I suggested. "Why don't you put that stuff down"—I moved my arm to indicate the gasoline and the matches—"come inside, I'll make you some cocoa, I know how much you like my cocoa, and we'll talk."

He shook his head. "No, Elmo. I don't want to talk, and I don't want any cocoa. I'm not thirsty." A brief pause, a grin, and yet another flash of wry amusement. "Are *you* thirsty, Elmo?"

"No," I answered. "I'm not thirsty."

He said nothing, and try as I might I couldn't read him. "Why don't you go and burn down that big house, Jeff," I said. "You might enjoy it."

He shook his head briskly. "My God, Elmo, I don't *enjoy* this. I do what I *have* to do." He paused, then added, "You know what the war did for me, Elmo?"

"No. What did it do for you?"

"It reaffirmed my belief in evil."

"I'm glad," I said.

"Do you believe in evil?"

"I believe in compulsion," I said.

"That's pretty slippery, Elmo. Very, very slippery." And he turned and walked quickly back to his little house.

Lemuel was found unconscious beside the car the next day, and the old priest, still in the passenger's seat, was crossing himself repeatedly and mumbling that a vampire was loose near Bridgeston. (I found out later, from Lemuel himself, that he had regained consciousness for about an hour, had looked in the passenger window and babbled on and on about me, which I like to believe was a function of his pride.) It's what the Bridgeston newspaper said: "LOCAL PRIEST CLAIMS VAMPIRE IN AREA"—which not even the townies professed to believe. They did not close their houses up tight, they did not lock their shutters or hang garlic here and there—which, because I long ago lost the sense of smell, has no effect on me anyway—crosses were not scrawled over doorways, holy water wasn't sprinkled about. Of course, none of the locals had any real idea what a vampire was. The vampire had not yet become a part of American popular mythology, so when that decrepit old priest began babbling about them, no one could do more than scratch his or her head. Until Hiram Shepard and Betty Singer appeared. "Get some holy water," they said. "Hang garlic," they said. "Keep your windows closed," they said. They even held a public meeting on the matter at the Bridgeston Grange Hall. The women brought cakes and cookies, the men brought their own home-made whiskey—which started a pang of the old hunger in me—and they all sat around fanning themselves against the mid-evening July heat while Hiram and Betty entertained them.

I was there. I sat in the back. I was wearing a light summer jacket with the collar turned up to hide my face—since I hadn't eaten in some time I was beginning to look a bit grim—and I think I must have smelled bad, too, because several people sat next to me briefly, wrinkled their noses and went to sit elsewhere.

Hiram and Betty had put together quite a show. They had a nice, ten-minute movie—in black and white, of course; this was 1928—that purported to show the origins of the vampire, beginning with that impossible fifteenth-century fraud, Vlad the Impaler, who got his kicks out of impaling his countrymen on long wooden poles and leaving them to rot.

And, after Vlad, the movie touched briefly on vampire folklore from around the world. Betty enjoyed pointing out that the "vampire legend" is not restricted to Eastern European countries, as some might think (and it pleased me to read the confusion that passed through the room then, because practically no one there knew what an "Eastern European country" was), but that, "indeed," she said, "the vampire leaves its stench on *all* humanity." Again there was confusion in the room.

A fat woman in her late forties who was wearing a dark blue dress that was sweat-stained on the back raised her hand, stood, and waited a few seconds for Betty to recognize her. When Betty failed to recognize her, the woman took the initiative and interrupted with, "These vampires? Are they teched or what, missus, 'cuz I got this boy at home what likes to do real *nasty* things to frawgs—"

And Betty cut in, "They are *obsessed*, ma'am."

"Obsessed? What's 'obsessed'?"

"They can't help themselves—"

"Oh, he feeds his-self all right—" the woman began, and Betty, realizing that neither she nor Hiram had mentioned the most salient point about vampires, announced, "Vampires are not *living* creatures, ma'am."

The woman thought about that a moment—which was as much time as her brain could devote to thought—and then chuckled, "So if they ain't *living creatures* then what in the sam hell we got to fear from 'em, missus, you want to tell me that?"

This made Betty uncomfortable. She glanced at Hiram, who was standing to one side, also uncomfortable. He glanced back at her, came forward, and intoned, "They are the walking dead."

The woman's head tilted slightly to one side. She smiled a flat, impatient smile, and said, her tone very instructive, "They can't *do* that, mister, I'm sorry, but they can't *do* that." And she sat down, plop, as if the whole matter had been forever set aside.

Hiram frowned. I heard the words, *This is not going well!* pass through his head, and for the very briefest

170

moment I got the urge to join him on stage and introduce myself. But then he said, surprising me, "It is possible that the vampire is here with us tonight."

Heads turned this way and that, there were a few guffaws, a few gasps, then a boy of about thirteen, with light blond hair, a large nose, thin lips and flat, piercing blue eyes levelled his gaze on me. The ghost of a grin appeared on his mouth, then flickered out. He nudged his mother, sitting beside him, and whispered to her, "He's over there, Maw, the vampire's over there!" But she didn't hear him and he didn't feel bold enough just then to repeat himself.

"And if he *is* here," Hiram went on, feeling that he had finally gotten the ear of his audience, "then he knows our strategy and so we must be especially vigilant." There was another wave of confusion—very few in the room knew what the words "strategy" or "vigilant" meant. So someone said, "You wanta talk American!"

"We must keep our guard up, dammit!" Hiram said, near the level of a shout. "Because if we don't then we will become his prey—"

"We all pray, mister," the same man said, and several of the others turned around and shushed him, obviously feeling the true weight of Hiram's words, at last.

But Hiram picked up on it. "As well you should, my friends," he said. "Pray loudly and long, keep your windows closed and your hearts pure, because it is the very devil himself that we are dealing with here."

I resented that. I *still* resent it. The devil has nothing to do with us.

171

So I took a chance. I raised my hand, waited for recognition, got it, and said, "*Men* are capable enough devils, Mr Shepard."

"Who's he?" someone whispered, and I immediately realized my mistake.

"Who's he?" someone else said.

"A stranger," someone answered.

And Hiram said, "That's an interesting observation, sir, would you care to elaborate on it?"

"No, I wouldn't," I whispered, stood very quickly, and pushed out of the room and into the night.

Behind me I heard, "It was him," and "It was the vampire"; then, in a voice that had the ring of authority to it, "Nope, it was just a stranger, it weren't no vampire," which quieted everyone.

17

———

It's not that I don't trust Jeff. I know, through what goes on in his brain, almost all of what there is to know about him, so I know pretty much what he's capable of, and what he's going to do from one moment to the next.

But he's confused, so it's a hell of a lot harder to read him than it is to read, for instance, the boy that I keep in the aluminum shed.

And, I'll admit it, Jeff may be *trying* to block me, may have some deep-seated and instinctive mistrust of me, may even *know* what I am, somewhere beneath his consciousness (far enough beneath it, in fact, that when the knowledge filters up to where he can verbalize it, his sense of reality and fair play has changed it considerably).

Wednesday

The boy at the Bridgeston Grange Hall lived with his mother in a small, wood-frame house within the Bridgeston town limits. His name was Andrew

McKeegan Jr. His mother's name was Jenny LouAnne McKeegan, and she was twenty-nine years old.

The house that she and her son lived in in Bridgeston had been built thirty years before by her late husband's father, Herbert McKeegan, and Jenny looked forward to living in it for the rest of her life. She hoped fervently, too, that her son would go on living in it with her. She was very possessive of him. She wasn't *proud* of him in the usual sense, she couldn't imagine that he'd end up as anything more important than a cannery worker, which his father had been, but she was possessive of him. It was an incestuous possessiveness, though she'd never have admitted it, even to herself, and, just as certainly, would have never done anything to satisfy it.

Andrew, to his credit, was aware of his mother's possessiveness, and understood it. She wanted him to take his father's place, eventually, in every area except the bedroom, because although Andrew McKeegan Sr had not been the most intelligent or enlightened of men—qualities which Jenny couldn't have cared less about, anyway—he was a good provider and without him or his son she had nightmares of having to sell herself merely to live. Andrew McKeegan Jr understood this, too—his instincts were superb—and so he had resigned himself to living life as a bachelor, taking care of his mother until she passed on.

Then he turned his head that night at the Bridgeston Grange Hall, saw me, nudged his mother, and said, "There he is, Maw." Because it was *he*, you understand, much more than Hiram Shepard or Betty Singer, who caused the people in Bridgeston to lock their doors and windows tight. And made me go hungry. Because he talked to his mother later, and she talked to her friends, and they talked to theirs, and within hours the fact of my continuing hunger was set in stone.

Little Andrew McKeegan Jr had to be taught a lesson. Little Andrew McKeegan Jr had to suffer much, much more than he had made me suffer (it was only fair).

The house had no cellar entranceway from within the house, itself. The cellar entrance was from the outside, through a set of double steel doors which Jenny never kept locked. Herbert McKeegan had built the house this way because cellar entrances, he maintained, were also perfect entrances for "bandits and thieves".

The night after the Bridgeston Grange Hall fiasco, I got in through those cellar doors, put myself in a far corner, near a huge multi-armed steam boiler that was working at full throttle, and waited. I have almost literally the patience of the dead—I could probably wait forever, and not care much.

I waited two days and nights. It was as I waited that I learned all that I have reported here about the McKeegans. I learned it through Jenny herself, whose thoughts flowed down to me like water from within the house.

Little Andrew McKeegan Jr loved his mother. I knew this as certainly as I knew anything else. He loved her because she had fed him all his life, and had held him close to her on certain nights, and because she was nice to look at, and her body was soft and comfortable. There are probably no better reasons to love someone. And it had never occurred to him that there might come a time when he would be without her, when someone would have to try and take her place, someone not quite so nice to look at, someone who spoke harshly to him, and told him, on certain nights, to be a big boy and go back to bed.

So when Jenny LouAnne McKeegan came into the cellar the third night after the Bridgeston Grange Hall fiasco, I knew exactly how I wanted to even the score with her son.

She was looking for a jar of raspberry preserves, and mumbling to herself, flashlight in hand, that she wished it wasn't so "gosh-awful dark". I let her look awhile; she found a jar and held it close to her face to read the label. From my corner of the cellar, near the steam boiler, I said, "Your son is very perceptive, Mrs McKeegan. Much too perceptive."

"Wha—?" she said, and repeated it almost at once, "Wha—?" and shone the flashlight in my direction. Its beam caught me first in the chest. She brought it quickly up to my face.

I said again, "Your son is much too perceptive, Mrs McKeegan."

"Who the hell are you?" she said with a noticeable tremor in her voice. "Speak up, now!" I had expected (from all that I had read from her in the previous two days) only a stiff, paralytic, and ignorant fear—the kind I read in small animals—but that wasn't what I got. I got anger, as if I were a young boy, like her son,

176

and had done something naughty. What I wanted most, I think, was *recognition*.

She said again, "Speak up, now!"

I moved slowly, with a grisly determination, out of my corner.

"You got somethin' wrong with you, boy?" she demanded.

I pretended a smile.

"Good Lord, boy—your *breath*!"

I was a good ten feet from her now, and still smiling. From above, I heard her son call to her, "Maw? Where are you, Maw?"

I looked up and said, "Your son is looking for you, Mrs McKeegan." My smile increased dramatically.

"Down here," she called. "Get the shotgun, Andrew!"

And I bellowed at her, "You have no idea at all who I am, do you, Mrs McKeegan?"

Her nose wrinkled up. "I know you smell bad."

"By Jesus, I am your eternal damnation!"

She chuckled. "And yer gonna be fulla holes if you don't get outa here right now!"

From above, her son called to her. "You in the cellar, Maw?"

"Get the shotgun, Andrew," she called again.

"Do you know what I'm going to *do* to you, Mrs McKeegan?" I said.

Then a small, quivering smile appeared on her lips. "Hey, you ain't that *vam*pire are you? Is that what you are? Lord Almighty . . ."

"Yes," I said, happy that at last she'd caught on to what was happening.

"And you honest to God believe that yer dead and gone?"

I shook my head slowly. "Not *gone*, Mrs McKeegan."

She turned her head and called, "Andrew, you got the shotgun? Whatchoo doin' up there?"

And I heard, from the cellar entranceway, "Yeah, I got it, Maw. Whatchoo want me to do?"

I was becoming annoyed and frustrated. It was clear that these people had no real appreciation for who or what I was. If I had been able to sigh, I would have. Instead I said to Mrs McKeegan, "I'm hungry. I am very hungry. And it's *you* I hunger for."

She said, chuckling again, "You got a good line, anyway." And added, without more than a second's pause, "Shoot him, Andrew."

Andrew balked. "Shoot him? You mean for real?"

She looked sharply at him, "He's a *tres*passer, Andrew. And *tres*passers get shot where I come from."

Andrew shook his head. "I ain't never actually shot no one, Maw—" He fired. It was probably a mistake. He got tense, his finger tightened. The trouble was, the shotgun wasn't aimed at me, it was aimed at that big, multi-armed steam boiler which was working at full throttle. And although Jenny LouAnne McKeegan would never have retreated from *me* until her throat was in my mouth, when that boiler got hit and miniature geysers started erupting everywhere, she screamed shrilly, dropped the jar of raspberry preserves, cursed, and headed for the exit. Her son—transfixed by what he had done to the boiler—blocked her way. "Gee," he whispered, "Gee, that's great, ain't it? That's great!"

She tried to push him up the cellar stairs. He resisted. She pushed harder, he fell, the shotgun clanked to the cellar floor. I moved to it, picked it up, took both ends of the barrel in my hand, held it up so Jenny and Andrew could see what I was doing, stared hard at the barrel, and bent it easily and theatrically into a U. I grinned, looked at where mother and son had been on the cellar stairs, saw nothing. "Fuck!" I whispered. They were gone. They hadn't even been watching.

I don't know if I could do that trick now.

I think Jeff was right. I think I'm shrinking. I think I'm getting smaller. And weaker.

18

———

Tonight, the night after Jeff wanted to burn this house, he said, "What are you, Elmo?"

We were in the library, he with his usual cup of cocoa in hand, and I with the same (although, remembering the incident with the coffee at his house, I merely touched the cup to my lips and never attempted to drink from it). He looked casual. I think it's the first time that he has not looked tense. Maybe he's getting used to his situation.

"I'm only what I appear to be, Jeff," I said to him.

He smiled a little, as if humoring me, and, reading him, I knew it was precisely what he was doing. "And tell me what you think you *appear* to be, Elmo."

"You tell me, Jeff."

He sipped his cocoa, liked it, sipped it again, set the cup on the floor beside his chair. "I don't know," he said, grinned, and added, "I don't know if I trust you."

"Or I you, Jeff," I said.

He was toying with me. I didn't like it.

He said, "Where did you tell me you came from, Elmo? Somewhere down south?"

"Hanford, Kentucky."

"Uh-huh," he said. "I've never been there, I've been to the Carolinas, but never to Kentucky." He stood and grinned his playful grin. He was still toying with me, or trying to. He said, "I've been to lots of places, but never to Kentucky." He went to the window, parted the curtain, peered out. He said, his back to me, "It's going to be a cold night, Elmo. I can feel it."

"Yes," I said.

"Might even be a frost. I hope you've got a good warm bed to sleep in."

"I do," I said.

He glanced around, grinned once more, let go of the curtain. "Do you?" he said. "That's good, Elmo, we wouldn't want you catching a chill, would we?"

"No," I said.

Moments later, he left.

If I had lived, and learned how to love, and been able to love, I believe that I would have loved a woman like Tad Hamilton. She speaks to me from every corner of this house, she says that she understands what I am, and wishes she could caress me.

And I wish she could.

19

I got Lemuel out of that prison, of course, and quite
easily, too. I hardly needed to be invited in, did I?
After all, who has ownership and tenancy of a prison?
The people do, the tax-payers. And though it is
technically true that I had never paid taxes in North
Carolina (technically, I had never paid taxes anywhere), it was hardly a psychic point against me. That
prison was mine as much as it was anyone else's. I
had as much right in it as Lemuel did. But he invited
me in, after all, which saved me some possible
embarrassment.

When I got him out (and I had to man-handle
several guards to do it, one a large, red-haired Irish-
man who continuously muttered small, Catholic
prayers from the corner of the cell where I tossed him),
we found a house several miles from the prison that I
liked very much because it seemed the proper place
for the creature I had become; it was big, damp, and
cold, Lemuel told me. And it had many rooms. (What
need was there to go further? Dogs can't track me,
dogs *refuse* to track me, and I knew that the authorities

expected we'd try to leave the state.) And it was in this house that I first encountered my ability to feel and experience the lives of those who have moved on (in the very liberal sense of the phrase—moved on to Kansas, moved on into death; it doesn't matter because they leave much of themselves behind wherever they go—good, bad, tacky, distasteful, the essence of what they are lingers after they've moved on, and I can feel it).

I knew that a family of murderers had once lived in the house I took Lemuel to.

Jeff is beginning to annoy me. He's found the boy in the shed and is keeping him in his house in a bedroom of his own, is feeding him, bringing him back, feels sorry for him. He thinks that I'm to blame for the state the boy is in, though he doesn't know precisely how. Again the phrase *Elmo is a dead man* runs about in his head, and I'm not sure if it's merely a statement of fact, or if it's a plan he's made—*Elmo's going to be a dead man*.

Thursday

But the boy died, that's the sense I get of it—that he died. Jeff blames me for it.

"Elmo, I found a small boy in an aluminum shed."

"Yes?" I wasn't about to let him into the house. I told him I was tired, that I was going to go to bed, so he stood at the bottom of the steps with his can of gasoline and his kitchen matches in hand, and though he was telling me something that should have been very tragic for him, I sensed that he was sniggering at me, fighting to keep himself from erupting into a fit of the giggles. "Some local boy?" I asked.

He shrugged. "Sure. Some local boy. I tried to help him. I fed him, I read to him—some kids' books I found in the house, Dr Seuss—Have you read Dr Seuss, Elmo?—and the Berenstain Bears, which I used to like when I was a kid, and I joked with him and told him I'd take care of him. I was even going to take him camping, Elmo—I found a tent and everything. But he died. Just like that." He snapped his fingers. "He died. I buried him out back of the house."

"Oh?"

"Did *you* kill him, Elmo?"

"How could I have killed him, Jeff?"

He shrugged. "I don't know, I thought you might have, that's all, it's not important."

"No," I said. "I didn't kill him."

"Nor did I," Jeff said, and turned and went back to his house.

The house several miles from the prison in North Carolina spooked the hell out of Lemuel—"Don't wanna stay here, Elmo," he said again and again. "Don't feel too good here, Elmo, feel like throwin' up here, in fact." And during our first night in it, he actually did throw up, though I was sure it was only because of a passing virus. But every night we were there, he got out of sorts at eight o'clock or so. It was, I could feel it, the proverbial "witching hour" in that house. It was when the best and the grisliest murders had been done. Murders too grisly even for poor Lemuel. (It surprised me that he developed some of the same psychic talents that I had. I have no explanation for it. I don't believe that he developed them *through* me somehow, through osmosis. I think it's more likely that he was born with those gifts, although while we were mortal friends he never displayed them.)

"Bad people, Elmo," he whispered to me every night at a little past eight, after his sessions of vomiting, and I told him, "Yes they were, Lemuel," though my concepts of bad and good seemed pretty much what I could gather together from memory, sort out, add up, subtract—as if on some great, dark abacus—and then, with a dollop of what served as morality from Lemuel's own consciousness, announce, "Yes, they were bad," or, "Yes, they were good." It kept up appearances. Even Lemuel needed to believe that there was still some humanity left in me. He was terribly human himself. He was fond of animals and small children, and, of course, his Norman Rockwell kind of Huck Finn look wasn't entirely at odds with his real character. He would have been happy as a clam to have spent his life fishing, sleeping, and making love. I miss his unchallenging and unquestioning companionship, and I sometimes wonder if he is not out there somewhere, beyond this village, an incredibly aged Huck Finn, still fishing and sleeping, and making love.

Saturday

The family of murderers who used to live in the house I took Lemuel to were very tidy, even fastidious, they spread doilies on everything, over the backs of couches and chairs, on tables, on the icebox, and they took baths two or three times a day, each of them long, very hot baths because they despised the odor of sweat, and always in privacy, never willing to display their nakedness to one another, not even the husband to the wife, the daughters to the mother, the sons to the father. These were profoundly disturbed people, and they did their murders twice a month.

I was entertained then, in that house, by the memory of those murders. I told Lemuel, in fact, that God had *invented* murder in order that it be done the way in which that family did it—with style and cruelty.

I told Lemuel that the people who had lived in the house were human vampires.

They were the Nelsons and they were all hanged, even the children, on the day before Christmas in 1919, from an aged and wonderfully gnarled oak tree that stood just south of the house, close enough, in fact, that several of its middle branches actually touched the house.

There were no ghosts in the house when Lemuel and I arrived. The world is cluttered with ghosts, of course, but in 1929 there were no ghosts in that house, only memories, and they were as strong and as hard as granite.

*

Jack Nelson was a banker. He was thirty-nine years old when the locals hanged him, and his wife was thirty-five, fair-skinned, petite, and pretty. Both her daughters were petite and pretty, too. They were named Megan, age seventeen, and Jane, age fifteen. The sons were younger but already looked much like their father, who was the picture of tanned and athletic good health. There were two sons, Robert and Marion, and on the Christmas Eve that they were hanged they were ten and thirteen years old, respectively. They also had a maid, a black woman named Henrietta Bodine, who participated in none of the murders, though she knew of them, and she was hanged much further from the house, on a tree not so wonderfully gnarled or aged as that oak, but which was stout enough to support her considerable weight. She was allowed to dangle from it for several weeks. The Nelsons were cut down on Christmas Day, which one of the locals deemed an "act of charity".

20

Sunday Evening

Jeff came to the house tonight and said that he wanted to talk, that he had some things to get off his chest, so I made him some cocoa and showed him into the library. We sat in our usual chairs.

I can't read him anymore. His mind is like blue sky one might try to find stars in—so I've grown distrustful of him. I think he's got something up his sleeve, I think he sees himself as some kind of magician— God's magician—so I have moved my sleeping place to a far corner of Tad Hamilton's cellar, into a room with a steel door and thick stone walls, and I've installed a hefty lock on the inside of the door.

"I like you, Elmo," Jeff said tonight, and sipped his cocoa delicately.

I nodded. "Thank you. It's good to be liked."

"It's good to have a *friend*, Elmo. Especially now."

"Now?" I said.

"Yes. I killed one of those survivalists today."

"Go on," I said.

"It was self-defense, of course. I had to do it." He

paused, glanced away briefly, glanced back, went on, "I killed the woman, Mrs Jarvis. I bashed her head in with a shovel." He sipped his cocoa again. "She was coming at me with a gun and she was babbling about vampires—*vampires*, Elmo—and she was dying, too. The radiation, I think. So when she got close enough I bashed her head in with a shovel and then I took the gun from her and put two bullets into her brain." Another pause.

"Go on," I said again.

He shrugged. "And I buried her out back of the house, near where I buried the little boy. I hated to do it, of course."

I said, "You're lying to me, Jeff." It was a stab in the dark.

He sipped his cocoa, stared into the cup a moment. "It's very cold in this house, Elmo," he said, and looked up at me. "Do you know that it's cold in here?"

I ignored the remark. "I don't believe that you killed Mrs Jarvis," I said. "I think you're trying to be entertaining."

This clearly amused him; he smirked. "Why would I want to *entertain* anyone, Elmo?"

"Because you're human," I answered, "and death entertains you." But he was still smirking, and I was becoming annoyed by it. "Don't smirk, Jeff," I said. He stopped at once.

"*Do* you feel the cold, Elmo?" he said.

I nodded. "Yes, I do. And I feel warmth, too. And I feel a very distinct coolness from you at this moment."

He said again, "I like you, Elmo. You're a survivor, like me." He stood, stretched. "Got to go. Sorry. I'm a little tired." He gave me a once-over. "Stand up, would you, Elmo."

"Why?" I said.

"It's nothing. It's just that you really do look . . . smaller. Are you sure you're getting enough to eat?"

"Yes," I said.

"Uh-huh," he said, grinned, added, "Well, you really do look *awful*," and quickly left the house.

When I sleep, I move off into shafts of wheat and into whitecaps and I become small boys, and snails, and I'm sure that when I sleep I am something that's holy, I believe I am consecrated, priestly, and I do not want the destruction of all that is because it would be the destruction of myself, which my hunger serves. I am creation, I am holy, and consecrated, and what I do is only what the tiger does, merely what the tiger does, no more than needs to be done for the sake of God, who gives me wrong answers from time to time, it is true, and then laughs at my clumsiness, but who is also a survivor, and so deserves a nod from me.

21

I could get away from Jeff, I could go into the city and lose myself. If I had to, I could feed on derelicts, although, on second thoughts, I imagine that the radiation has gotten most of them. I wonder sometimes if it has had any effect on me. I'd guess that it hasn't. Still, in many ways I'm completely physical—my bones can snap and my skin peel away, though I wouldn't know it. I need to see myself through someone else's eyes now, through Jeff's eyes, but I can't because I can't read him anymore, and except for the eyes of the rats and the birds, I am blind.

Jack Nelson's real name was William Nelson the Third. He hated his parents so he dropped half his name and called himself Jack, which they despised.

  He and Myrna were married when he was twenty-two and still in college. They looked forward to a quiet life, nice kids, getting old and tired together, and smiling at their grand-children. Then Jack did a murder one night. It wasn't premeditated or particularly heinous (he could, in fact, have easily convinced a jury that it was self-defense), but it was something that he enjoyed more than he had ever enjoyed anything, even more, he realized with a little shudder, than he enjoyed sex.

It was very quick. It was done literally before he knew that it was done. And when the body lay at his feet he realized that he had found his calling, that he had stumbled, at last, upon his life's work—to be a murderer. It made him very happy.

(Without Jeff's eyes to see through, or the boy's, or one of the survivalists'—who seem very distant—I see through the eyes of rodents and birds. There aren't many birds left, but the rodents have survived and they feed on the dead, of course. The rodents are everywhere, and it's more often than not *their* eyes I see through. But the perspective sometimes confuses me, as does the lack of color, and the constant movement is irritating, so I've gotten the idea of trapping one of them and trussing it up. Then I'd have its captive eyes to see through.)

The rooms in Jack Nelson's house were done in a wide variety of colors. Yellow predominated in the hallways on all three floors—a bright, canary-yellow on the first floor, a noticeably darker, almost school-bus-yellow on the second floor, an unpleasant, dark orange-yellow on the third floor. All twenty of the rooms followed this ascending light-to-dark motif, the impression being, of course, that correspondingly darker crimes were committed on the upper two floors. The painting had clearly been done by professionals, I could see no brush strokes, no uneven lines, no drips here and there on the floors, which were a highly polished dark oak. And when Lemuel and I came to the house it had gone untouched ever since the Nelsons had been strung up behind it ten years before, because it was, quite naturally, an incredibly forbidding house, not at all entertaining even to look at, as presumably most haunted houses are. I imagined that even the local adolescent boys gave it a wide berth, though on that score (and sadly for the particular adolescent boy) I was wrong.

We would like most to remember only the good things. Especially when we begin to feel that the houselights are coming down. But too often the bad creeps in.

I visited Jeff tonight at his house. He was sitting in front of the TV, which he'd switched on, although the screen was blank, of course. I sat across from him, and he said, "I'm going to start shooting the rats, Elmo."

And I said, "They're part of the system, Jeff. They help dispose of the dead." I would have been blind there, in his house, had it not been for a garden spider in a window behind me—the images I saw through its eyes were misshapen, and dark, but recognizable.

Jeff chuckled. I was hearing him through the house itself, through the mice that lived in the walls and ceiling. "I don't like rats, Elmo. I've always shot rats, I shot rats when I was a kid. I shot mice, too. And bats. That was tricky because bats move so goddamned fast. Have you ever seen one flying, Elmo?"

"No," I said.

"They fly like this," he said and moved his hand erratically in the air. He grinned, let his hand drop. "So you've got to get off a good spray of shot at them. I used my father's twenty-gauge and I hardly ever missed—I must have blown ten thousand of the little bastards straight back to hell, Elmo. Christ I hated them. That's why I'm going to shoot the rats."

I said nothing. He was beginning to make me uncomfortable, and he knew it.

After a moment, he said, "That's the trick, Elmo. You've got to get off a good spray of shot at them. The bastards don't die easy; one little bitty pellet's not going to do the trick. A hundred pellets, a full load of shot—for the love of God, Elmo, it really tears them up, and if you're good, if you're very, very good, and your aim is true, and the rat is big enough, sometimes, with the right pattern of shot, you can actually tear their hides away and leave them alive. Skinned and squeaking. Then you can put them out in the sunlight and watch them bake." A short pause, then he went on, his tone a little lighter, "Shit, that's something we can do together one of these days, Elmo, we can go shooting the rats. How'd you like that? Do you think you'd like that?"

"It sounds pretty grisly," I said.

He chuckled. "It does sound grisly, doesn't it? But to tell you the truth, I've never shot anything. I've never even *fired* a gun, Elmo." He shrugged. "Let the rats do their work. We *all* have to do our work, we've got to get civilization moving again, isn't that right? I mean, where are we without the vote, Elmo? Where are we without Tupperware, and free elections?"

Another chuckle—I heard a dozen or more of them in very rapid succession, nearly in unison, because I was hearing them through a dozen or more ears— then he continued, "What do you think of that?"

I said, "I don't know what Tupperware is, Jeff."

We don't remember only the good. I remember Jack Nelson's house. I remember Lemuel. But I remember my father, too, and I remember him looking out at me that cold Christmas Eve.

After a moment Jeff added, "You know, of course, Elmo, that you're not looking at me, you're looking straight at my elbow. Why are you doing that? You've been doing it ever since you got here. And you don't *move* very much, either. I don't think you move at all. I hardly think you're breathing."

A very brief pause, then he said, "Thanks for coming, Elmo. You can go now."

The particular adolescent boy who came to Jack Nelson's house in 1929 shortly after Lemuel and I got there was thirteen years old, had bright red hair and a splash of freckles across his nose. He was very pale, and he was also unutterably frightened in that house.

"What's your name, boy?" I asked him. He was at the opposite end of the second-floor hallway, a distance of nearly fifty feet, but my voice moved well and powerfully in it.

"Orry," he answered. I'll give him credit, he didn't stutter, his voice was strong and sure.

"Why are you here?" I asked, and I took several steps toward him. The light wasn't good in that hallway. Through his eyes I could see that his image of me was of a tall, gaunt, and darkly dressed man whose face seemed no more than a cream-colored blur, which doubled his fear, of course.

"I can go," he suggested, his voice still unusually strong. He backed away a step or two, hesitated, turned toward the stairway.

"No reason to go, Orry."

"Sure is," he said, and he was gone.

And when he saw me, two or three seconds later, grinning maliciously at him from the bottom of the stairway, my face was much clearer to him (thanks to Lemuel, who lived on the first floor and kept several lights burning because he didn't like the darkness very much), and he backed away, up the stairs. I went after him, caught him, grabbed him by the hair, yanked him down the stairs—he was screaming all the while—felt his young bones snapping as his body flailed about (this was not unlike the feeling I used to get back home in Hanford when I snapped fresh corn on the cob for cooking). I supposed that I might even have been cackling, I was so delighted. Like a cat with a chipmunk, I wanted to *play* with this boy. But my compulsion got the better of me and I took my fill of him. I felt his pain and anguish, and his grief at his own death, and I read in him that there were others like him, young adolescent boys waiting for him beyond the house somewhere, not close by. One of these boys was his younger brother, and one was his cousin. And reaching out to them I knew that they were already planning a good excuse for the disappearance of Orry—that they'd all gone swimming at the local swimming hole and that Orry had gone under and had never come up—because they weren't supposed to be *there*, at the Nelson house, and if anyone found out they were there then the punishment would be severe indeed. One of those boys was even planning on going to the Nelson house in search of Orry, because he was Orry's friend.

Then Orry died and his spirit went off, just as the spirits of the people in this village went off, in answer to a summons I have never heard.

The boy who was Orry's friend never came back to the Nelson house.

22

And for all I know, poor red-haired Orry is still in Jack Nelson's house, right where I left him, his snapped young bones bleached clean by time.

We do not live forever. None of us wants it and none of us achieves it. The hard and simple fact is that immortality would be an excruciating bore. *Compulsion* becomes a bore after a while—for some of us after only a couple of decades. That's the way it was with Lewis Perdue, at the University of North Carolina at Chapel Hill. He taught a night class in English Literature, and we recognized each other instantly as members of the same species, which was wonderful. I'd been without the companionship of my own kind for nearly two years, ever since Regina Watson and I had stood side by side in those piney woods and had watched the snow fall. But she had been less than rational. She'd gotten locked tooth and claw into being the archetypal vampire, and she quickly became what her son had become (because he'd had so little time learning to be human)—a wide-eyed, quivering, and insatiable mass of fears and compulsions which, because of its own needs, eventually dooms itself. Which is probably the fate of most of us.

Lewis was short, a little chunky (and this led me to believe that in life he must have been obese), had very dark brown hair, a round, pleasant face, large, tear-shaped, brown eyes, and the beginnings of a mustache (which never got finished, of course). He spoke with the hint of a Brooklyn accent, and I learned that he had indeed come from Brooklyn, had been born there, raised there, went to City College, taught there for several years, and, in 1923, in a grimy, harshly lit, eight-stool diner, he met an old woman dressed in a faded black dress and tattered wool coat. She told Lewis she needed some help getting home.

I knew that Lewis Perdue was one of my own kind because he was the only one in that classroom at Chapel Hill whom I couldn't read. We cannot read each other. I have no idea why. And because *I* was the only one in the room that *he* couldn't read he knew precisely what I was and it made us both exquisitely happy.

So, that first flirtatious nod which passed between us is something that I'll always cherish.

We went on a spree together, and when we were done at least a half dozen of Chapel Hill's best and brightest had fallen. One or two had been transformed.

We were very selective about whom we transformed. We thought of it as a rare gift, and so only the *very* best and the *very* brightest there at Chapel Hill would do because they were the ones, after all, who'd react to vampirism the way we had—with intelligence, grace, and, I'll admit it, some lingering traces of humanity. There were already far too many like Regina Watson and her son extant, creatures who had not bothered to learn subtlety or style, and the real danger in them lay in the fact that they were so damned *public* about what they did, which invited destruction on the rest of us—like the marauding lion who kills one too many natives and so clears the way for the wanton killing of the rest of its own kind.

Lewis and I discussed this often and at length in a small, out-of-the-way restaurant close to the university (it reminded him of the diner where he met the old woman in the wool coat) while we both pretended to nurse cherry phosphates all evening long (we always left a good tip so the waitress wouldn't complain that we never ordered anything to eat).

"We aren't *evil* in the sense that we kill unnecessarily," Lewis said once.

"Unless it's for sport," I said.

"Yes." A long, slow nod of the head. "Yes. Sport. Well, it keeps us sane, doesn't it? So of course it's necessary. No one curses the lake that someone drowns in merely because it's deep."

"I understand that," I said.

"You're very smart, Elmo. *We* are God's creatures as much as the barracuda is, as much as the dandelion is, and we do His bidding."

This was my first encounter with that kind of

thinking and it surprised me. He went on, "Does that astonish you, Elmo?"

"It does," I said.

"Are you saying that you don't believe it?"

"I wasn't aware that I was allowed to *believe* anything anymore, Lewis."

He attempted a grin; on him, it was almost convincing. "*Allowed*, Elmo? Allowed by whom? You're allowed to think because you *do* think, and you are allowed to believe for precisely the same reason. The fact that you are no longer human has nothing to do with it. You can appreciate what is beautiful, too. And if beauty, now, isn't quite the same thing it was when you were alive, then that's hardly your concern, is it? Because you can't do anything about it. Personally, I find that a pulsing jugular is every bit as beautiful as a Rembrandt or a first volume of Shakespeare was to me in life. And that does not imply, Elmo, that Rembrandt and Shakespeare are not still excruciatingly beautiful to me. They are. Perhaps more so, in fact, than they were when I was alive, because I can see them now with an incredibly heightened sense of . . . *existence*. Do you understand that?"

"No," I said.

Another long, slow nod. "You will," he said. "In time."

And now, of course, I do. And I think I miss Lewis even more than I miss Lemuel. I think I miss him almost as much as I miss life itself.

*

"I've been shooting the rats, Elmo," Jeff said.

"You told me you'd never fired a gun," I said.

It was just past sunset and I had walked into the village. It's all but gone now, Jeff has burned most of the houses and most of the shops.

I've done what I had planned to do; I've found a small rat and have trussed it up. I carry it around in a wicker basket that I found in Tad Hamilton's house. I've installed a rectangular screen in the front of the basket, the rat sees through it, and I see through the rat, sort of a seeing-eye rat, I guess, and I hear through his ears, too. He has incredible hearing.

"What's that, Elmo?" Jeff asked, nodding at the basket.

"It's a wicker basket."

"And what have you got in it?"

"A rat," I said.

He grinned. "Why do you carry a rat around in a wicker basket?"

"An eccentricity," I said.

"Uh-huh. Well, I'm sorry, Elmo, but I'm going to have to shoot the rat," and with those words he took a small calibre pistol out of his back pocket and pointed it at the wicker basket. The rat's eyes levelled on the barrel of the pistol and for a brief moment I was back in Hanford, staring down the barrel of a shotgun one of our neighbors had shot his wife with and was intent on shooting me with, too.

"The rat needs to live, Jeff," I said, and, my God, I think there was an element of pleading in my voice.

Jeff put the gun away. "Of course he does, Elmo.

We all do. Even you." Then he turned and wandered off. The rat lost him in the darkness.

I had come to the village in search of food. I didn't find any. I went back to Tad Hamilton's house and thought about my father staring at what he told himself was a tree stump at the front of his piney woods on Christmas Eve eighty years ago.

My rat has gone to sleep. My God, he has dreams, the rat has *dreams*, he dreams about being a baby rat. He dreams about suckling at his mother's teats. He dreams about being able to scurry from place to place, about feeding on the dead.

I have killed the rat and have found another one with better eyes.

23

Jeff came to the house late this evening, and perhaps it's the way I have to see him now, and hear him, but he seems bigger, stronger, louder, more abrasive than when we first met.

I led him into the library, got him some cocoa. He sat down with it and said, "We killed all the tigers a long time ago, Elmo—long before the war could have done it for us."

"Yes," I said. "I'm aware of that." I put the wicker basket beside my chair.

"We killed the wolves, too," he continued, "and the grizzly bears, and the eagles. They were crowding us out, don't you think?"

"I was never much of a naturalist," I said.

"Now we've got only the rats, Elmo. And the pigeons."

"And us," I said.

"Us?" He grinned a wide, patronizing grin. "There's no *us*. There's *me*."

I attempted a grin. "And me, Jeff," I said, trying very hard for a tone of grim determination.

Jeff sipped his cocoa. The rat closed its eyes for several seconds and I became blind. I heard Jeff say, into the darkness, "You are passé, my friend. We've proven that." Then I heard him stand, heard him set his cup down, and when the rat opened its eyes, I saw that Jeff was gone.

For the first time in eighty years I feel exhaustion settling over me.

In 1930, Lewis Perdue stripped himself naked, threw himself into the bright, October, noon-day sunlight, and was baked clean through to his bones in two hours. The authorities tried to gather him together and put him on a stretcher but he disintegrated in their hands like old newsprint, so they swept him up with a push broom and later on, much later on, someone wrote that he was a classic case of "spontaneous burning", and followed that with much pseudo-scientific speculation about why some people, "like Lewis Perdue," simply "burn themselves out from within." No one ever guessed that he was merely a vampire who'd gotten bored and had decided to give up the ghost.

I miss Lewis Perdue. Sometimes I wonder if he's gone off to the same place that the villagers have gone off to, and Orry, whose bones are doubtless still in Jack Nelson's house.

"You've got to have a hell of an ego to go on being a vampire," Lewis said to me once. "And I don't think mine is quite well-developed enough. It never was, even in life. Oh, I love the killing, I can't *help* that, we are on top of it when we kill, aren't we?"

"Yes," I said.

"And if all I had to do for the rest of my days was kill I'd probably be very contented. But I have to sleep, too, I have to go inside myself, and it's so damned *empty* in there, Elmo."

I nodded. I wasn't quite sure, then, in the last quarter of 1930, several weeks before he destroyed himself, that I knew precisely what he meant.

"Like being buried in sand, what can you do?" he went on. "You can't *do* anything. And if you try to remember the good times they're like someone else's, and in fact they are. They're not ours. What are we? We're nothing but gullets and teeth, Elmo."

I don't feel hunger much anymore. Mostly I feel exhaustion. And it is not the kind that sleep cures.

I see through the eyes of the rat. I didn't always see that way. In Jack Nelson's house I saw through my own eyes because my spirit was young, and exquisitely strong—it could soar, it could burrow, it could change, it could *become* the rat if it wanted, it could *become* poor red-haired Orry whose bones snapped so easily.

And, goddamnit, it's not that *I* have aged or changed or have been transformed. The world has.

*

Some of Lewis's last words to me were: "See that pretty young thing there, Elmo?" We were in the tiny restaurant that reminded him so much of the restaurant in the Bronx where he met the old woman in the tattered wool coat.

"Yes," I said. He had nodded at a woman in her early twenties who was standing across the street waiting for the light to change. It was early autumn, past sunset, and the light of a streetlamp to the right of the woman was throwing her shadow crisply onto the sidewalk and at an angle over the curb onto the street.

"I could leave this restaurant now," Lewis said. "And I could follow her. I could seduce her. I could kill her. The idea is very stimulating, in fact. And if I decided to do it, there would be nothing at all that she could do to stop me. And nothing I could do about it, either, even if I wanted to."

We watched her cross the street, turn right, and disappear into the darkness. Then Lewis said, "Not long ago, I would have done it. I would have had no choice. But now I find that I do have a choice. I can choose to stay here with you and ignore my hunger." He glanced reflectively at his glass of cherry phosphate. After a minute he went on, "It's what I choose to do, in fact. And that scares the hell out of me, Elmo."

I nodded, got up, left the restaurant, and sought out the "pretty young thing", as Lewis called her. I seduced her, easily enough, into someone's open garage.

"My name is Elmo," I told her. "I have a need for you."

She said nothing. I read fear in her—the same kind of stiff, paralytic fear that I had expected from Jenny LouAnne McKeegan, and it pleased me. I took hold of her shoulders, put my canines on her throat. And became aware that Lewis was just behind her. I moved my head back, away from her throat. "Hello, Lewis," I said.

"You are exceedingly good at doing what you must do," he said.

"Yes," I said. "I am."

"And what are you going to occupy yourself with when you're done with her?" he asked.

"I'll find someone else."

"And after that?"

"It will be morning, then. I'll sleep."

He nodded at the young woman. "Several years ago, before you became what you are—maybe you can remember that, Elmo—you would have made love to her, and perhaps there would have been as much pleasure for you in that as there is now in killing her."

"I don't think so, Lewis."

A pause for effect. Then, "You will, Elmo." And he was gone. I never saw him again.

Dear Lewis. I believe you now.

Today, while I slept, I heard a woman singing, as if she were calling to me from a great distance. It was an extraordinarily beautiful sound, and it lasted for several seconds, long enough that I knew that I had heard it before. It stopped abruptly, as if someone had closed a door between the woman and me to keep us apart.

24

The last time I saw Lemuel he had gotten rid of his Huck Finn overalls and his faded shirt and had bought himself a Sears three-piece suit.

We were staying just outside Baltimore at the time, in a small, cream-colored house on a dead-end street. Lemuel had rented the house several months earlier with money he'd lifted from several of my victims because for thirty years we had drifted from one abandoned farmhouse to another, all over the south (and once even up into Pennsylvania, which Lemuel despised—"Snooty northerners!" he said), and he had been complaining fiercely about not "havin' a home of my own, Elmo," for the last ten of those years.

The house had a crawl-space basement, and that's where I spent my days while Lemuel, I found out later, went in search of a job. It was when he appeared sporting his three-piece suit that I suspected our relationship was coming to an end.

"Gotta find my own way in the world, Elmo," he said. "I ain't gettin' no younger, ya know."

"Nor am I," I said.

He shook his head and grinned his big, stupid grin (although, I'll admit, it had grown less stupid through the years and, at last, even had some worldliness in it). "That ain't true, Elmo. Maybe you ain't gettin' no younger, but you ain't gettin' no older, neither."

I nodded. "And I can do the same for you, Lemuel."

"Nope. I mean, maybe you can, but you ain't gonna, 'cuz I been with you a long time, Elmo, and I seen what you gotta do, and I'm here to tell ya that you are God-awful pathetic sometimes, *God-awful* pathetic, and there ain't no way in hell"—another grin—"I wanta be like that! Shit, Elmo, I'd rather they shovel the dirt over me than be like that. So I got this suit here, nice, huh"—he strutted a bit; in thirty years he had aged, of course, but not dramatically, and his body was still trim, even vaguely athletic-looking—"I got it at Sears, Elmo, you oughta get yourself some stuff there, those clothes you're wearing are lookin' mighty grim."

"I'll give it some thought, Lemuel."

He shrugged. "And anyway, I been lookin' through the paper and there's all kindsa jobs. There's a job sellin' used cars over in Dundotton, and that's somethin' I'd surely like to do, 'cuz you know how good I am with cars, Elmo, and with people, too—"

"What are you telling me, Lemuel?"

"Tellin' you? I'm tellin' you I'm gonna go and get me a job sellin' cars." Another grin, and this time it was laced amply with savvy. "I'm tellin' you I don't need you no more. Fuck, Elmo, I'm closin' in on bein' *fifty* years old and what I got to show for bein' that old? I got a long line of dead people behind me callin' my name, tellin' me how worthless I am, that I ain't got no future." He was beginning to speak very succinctly, and it surprised me because it betrayed a kind of resolve that I had *never* suspected in him, I had always thought of him as big, stupid, and obscenely loyal, and there, in that little house outside Baltimore, he had become something else entirely. He had become a man in search of himself. Looking back, I think I would have been proud of him had I not been so angry.

"I'm sorry, Lemuel. I can't let you leave me. I need you."

He grinned yet again. "Sure you do, Elmo. I know you do."

I could not read him. I tried; I felt myself wrap around him, but I couldn't reach into him, and it made me angry. "Goddamn you, Lemuel—"

"*Fine* three-piece suit, Elmo. Lord, I'm gonna sell *lots* of fine new cars with my fine three-piece suit. Can you see me now? Can you see the old bitties with their fox furs comin' in there and seein' me with my three-piece suit?" He began to strut again. "Lordy, Elmo, they gonna be fallin' all over me!"

"It's not going to happen, Lemuel. I'm not about to let you leave me."

Another shrug. "You got to, Elmo, 'cuz I'm stronger than you."

"You're insane. You're *stupid* and you're insane."

"I may be stupid, Elmo. Shit, I *know* how stupid I am. But I gotta tell you this, I ain't insane, I ain't crazy, I ain't got no toys in my attic. I'm jus' lots stronger than you." And with that he went and

211

plopped himself in a big, red over-stuffed chair. We were in the living room, and the only furniture there was that red chair, a knotty pine coffee table that Lemuel had picked up at an auction, a floor-standing lamp in need of a shade, and an oil painting of a topless Spanish woman. Lemuel liked to stare at it for long periods of time.

I said again, "You're insane, Lemuel. Stupid and insane."

He shook his head briskly. "Nope. Sorry, Elmo."

"Damn you!" I hissed.

"Not me, Elmo. You, maybe. But not me. I'm stronger than you, lots stronger than you."

"What in the hell are you talking about?"

He tilted his head to one side, questioningly. "You mad at me, Elmo? You gonna hurt me, kill me? You cain't kill me. You're *dead*, Elmo." And then, I swear, he chuckled at me. "You're dead, and ain't nothin' no dead man can do to a man like me."

For the first time in thirty years I was beginning to have some respect for his abominable stupidity. "I can tear you apart, Lemuel, you *know* that."

He shook his head. "I don't know that, Elmo. Shit, you had to go and die to get to likin' the taste of blood—you had to go and *die* to like it, so fuck you, Elmo, and fuck Regina and fuck Jack Nelson and fuck Lewis Perdue, I'm gonna go sell some cars."

Moments later he was out the door and had disappeared into the night.

He had taken me by surprise, of course. Some creature, God perhaps, had given me a fistful of wrong answers—*Lemuel's an idiot!* he had told me, and

Lemuel's weak, Lemuel's just a puppy dog!—so Lemuel had been able to take me by surprise. While God laughed.

I let him go. Maybe there was still some affection lingering in me for him, or perhaps I was simply glad to get rid of him—no one needs to share his existence with a fool. But, even today, I like to believe that he's alive somewhere, still wearing that Sears three-piece suit, and still operating under the delusion that he is somehow stronger than I am.

25

In Hanford, eighty years ago, I liked Rebecca most of all. She seemed so approachable, so *good*, and so worthy.

We went to school together in Hanford. No more than fifty children were ever in the building at one time, although it was very large (the town fathers had expected an influx of new residents because it was rumored that the railroad was going to be diverted to Hanford, though it never was).

The school was a three-storey red brick building that had a boxy, straightforward, utilitarian look; it was flat, and ugly, a thousand others identical to it are probably still standing throughout the country.

Rebecca and I found many places to go and fool around in. Whole classrooms on the second and third floors were never used, so at regular intervals—usually just before the start of the school day and just after—we'd go into one of these rooms and spend a good twenty minutes fondling each other.

Three years after my transformation I went back to that school. Nostalgia took me back, I think. Lemuel was with me. It was well after midnight, sometime in July, and we had no trouble at all getting in.

Lemuel was confused. "Why you wanta come in here, Elmo?" We were making our way to the stairs that led to the second floor. I knew that the building wasn't empty; I knew that in one of the rooms the janitor had fallen asleep on the floor.

"Nostalgia," I said.

"What's that, 'nostalgia'?"

"It's wanting to go back." We got to the stairs. I stood at the bottom and looked up.

"Well, you are back," Lemuel said, still confused. "An' it's awful spooky here, damn, but it's spooky—"

"Don't be an ass, Lemuel."

The janitor woke. He was a very sensitive man, very alert, and even though he was at the other end of the building from us, he called out, "Who's dere? Someone dere?" which filtered down to us through the wide hallways as little more than an incoherent whisper.

"Elmo, I heard somethin'," Lemuel said.

"Of course you did," I said, and started up the stairs to the second floor.

Lemuel said behind me, "There's someone *here*! Damnit, Elmo, we gotta go!"

I said nothing. After a few moments, Lemuel followed me up the stairs. "'Nostalgia', Elmo? That's what brung you back here to this school? 'Nostalgia'? I never went to no school, you know that?"

"Shut up, Lemuel." He shut up.

"Who's dere?" the janitor said again. "Someone dere? Answer me, now."

I nodded to my right. "I want you to go and deal with the man coming down the hall toward us, Lemuel."

"He a big man? I don't feel up to messin' with no big man tonight, Elmo. I'm about dog-tired—"

"No, he's a small man. And he's old."

Lemuel nodded, looked back down the stairs. "Sure," he said, and went to find the janitor.

I sought out the last room that Rebecca and I had used. Room 214. I pushed the door open, stepped in. I saw that the desks had been taken away, that the room was empty, except for a pair of tattered black shoes in one corner, and a tall, metal locker in another, near the windows.

Lemuel appeared a couple of minutes later. He was breathing heavily, and he steadied himself with his hands on the doorjamb. After a few moments, he said, "He was a tough little bastard, Elmo, real wiry, you know, but he's all taken care of—was a friend of my daddy's, name is Leland Bohannon, and he and my daddy used to go fishin' and drinkin' together. Hell, Elmo, I guess he used to bounce me on his knee when I was a infant, though I don't remember that, of course, and he didn't recognize me, I guess. Oh maybe a little, maybe I seen somethin' in those tiny brown eyes a his like he know'd who I was, but he ain't about to tell nobody—"

"Shut up, Lemuel." He shut up, except to say, nodding at the empty room, "This where you did it to her, Elmo?" and he grinned.

"We never 'did it'," I told him. "We only . . . touched each other."

" 'Touched each other'? What's that? That almost like doin' it?"

"You're damned ignorant, aren't you, Lemuel?"

Another grin, as if in self-satisfaction. "Yeah, I am dumb, Elmo. The day is long and I am dumb."

But I look back, now, eighty years later, and I realize the chances are very good that poor Lemuel is rotting somewhere. And I think I almost feel sadness for him because I don't believe he was quite as ignorant as he professed. He might even have managed to sell a few cars there in Dundotton. He might even have managed to make some kind of life for himself without me.

Jeff said, standing on the front porch of the house, "Why won't you let me in, Elmo, are you afraid of me?" and I assured him that I was afraid of very little, him least of all.

"Good, then you'll let me in."

"No," I said. "I can't." It was close to daybreak; behind Jeff, to the east, the sky was beginning to lighten, a layer of low clouds was turning cream-colored.

Jeff nodded at the wicker basket I was carrying. "You're awfully attached to your little friend, aren't you, Elmo? Why is that?"

"He's good company," I answered.

"Better company than I am, Elmo?"

"No."

"Are you a snob, Elmo?"

"No."

"I think you're a snob. You'd let me in if you weren't."

"I can't let you in, Jeff. I've got to sleep—"

"Yes, of course you do." He grinned. "I'd say you need all the sleep you can get, Elmo, my friend, you don't look well. You look like crap, in fact. Go, look at yourself"—another grin—"and then come back here and tell me that you don't look like crap."

"I'm aware of what I look like, Jeff."

"I don't think so," Jeff said. "I don't think you have any idea at all what you look like. If you did I think you'd go crawl into someplace that was very dark"—he grinned—"and I think you'd stay there forever and ever."

"I'm aware of what I look like," I said again.

He shrugged. "Maybe you are," he said. He turned and started back to his house. "You're not very bright, Elmo," he called, and chuckled to himself. "See you later."

I was in the men's restroom of a thruway restaurant when the war started. I had gone there to get out of the late afternoon sunlight. I'd been spending the past dozen days or so in an abandoned and boarded-up fruit-stand close to the thruway near a town called Friend, and I was awakened from sleep by a young boy and a young girl. They had decided it would be a good idea to break into the fruit-stand for no better reason than that no one else had ever broken into it.

It was the little girl who saw me first. A quivering smile broke out on her face and she turned to the little boy and said, "Hey, I think there's a dead person in here." The little boy crowded her out of the way, stuck his head in through the opening they'd made, and, in the best Hammer Films tradition, I grabbed him by the throat with my right hand and hissed at him, "Get *out* of here, and take the light with you!" Then I pushed him hard enough that he tumbled backwards several times, and he and the little girl ran off screaming shrilly about the "bogeyman".

Several minutes later I had scrambled out of the fruit-stand and was in that thruway restroom, with the lights off.

Someone came in minutes later. "Hey, the lights are out," he said, though there was no one with him, and he felt for the switch and flicked the lights on. "Who wants to pee in the dark?" he murmured.

From the far stall I pleaded with him, "Please turn the lights out. I have car sickness."

He said, "Car sickness in a men's room?" and laughed.

"The light bothers me, please turn it out."

"Wait till I'm done here, would ya?"

Someone else came in, took up a position next to the first man; the first man said, "Guy over there says he's car sick, wants me to turn the lights off. You think he's a faggot?"

The second man shrugged, said, "So what if he is?" paused and added, "Did you hear about the explosion in St Louis? Some kind of nuclear explosion, I guess—one of the old nuclear plants, maybe."

And the first man said, "No, I didn't hear about

that," zipped himself up, and left. The second man called to me, "Are you okay, my friend?"

"Could you turn the lights out, please," I said. "I have car sickness." He turned the lights out and left.

When I came out of that restroom much later in the evening I saw bumper-to-bumper traffic on the thruway and I heard phrases like, "Just when I was going to get a promotion, too," and, "I hope the cat will be okay," and, "At least they didn't have to suffer," and, "Well, it's us or them, that's all!" These phrases were being bandied about by the occupants of the cars, and, in total, I think the mood was close to festive, like Mardi Gras.

I was standing in front of the thruway restaurant. Around me, people were hurrying in and hurrying out. One of them, a nattily dressed man in his early twenties, who had the glow of youth and health about him, glanced at me and said, "This is really something, isn't it?"

"What's really something?" I asked.

"This war, of course," he answered. "No more complacency now, right?" and without waiting for an answer he went into the restaurant.

Two patrolmen pulled up then, got out, approached me: "Got some ID, fella?" one of them said.

"No," I said. "I didn't know I needed it."

"You do," the other one said. "Come with us, please," and he took me by the arm.

"I'm under arrest?" Something that was close to amusement pushed through me. "You're arresting me? Don't you have to read me my rights? What's the charge?"

The one holding my arm pulled a slip of paper out of his pocket and began reading me my rights while the other one said, "A man answering your description was seen leaving the scene of a child molestation this afternoon."

"But there's a war on," I said.

The patrolman shook his head. "That's no concern of ours, we've still got a job to do," and, very amused now, I let them lead me to their car, handcuff me, and put me in the back seat.

They didn't get far with me, of course. They pulled onto the thruway, and came to a halt in the bumper-to-bumper traffic. I slipped out of the cuffs and tore them both apart. And when I got out of the car I became aware of a bright orange-blue glow at the northern horizon and I heard a man in the car next to the patrol car say, in awe, "Wow, look at that!" Then he turned his head and looked into the back seat. "Look at that, kids," he went on, very excited now. "That must be Buffalo!"

26

Being here is like being blind drunk. My eyes are the eyes of the rat trussed up in its wicker basket beside the chair, its gaze on a big window to my right that looks out on the village.

This rat's eyes are better than the eyes of the first rat. Its long-range vision is extremely acute and I can see what I would guess is a hawk circling some distance off in the dusk, far behind the Mumford Free Methodist Church (one of the few buildings that Jeff has not yet put to the torch), and I can feel a fleeting panic in the rat because it instinctively knows that it is food for the hawk.

I hear through the rat's ears. I hear insects scurrying about beneath the floor of the house; I hear the window glass cooing in a soft breeze. I hear the heartbeat of the rat, like water dripping rapidly on wood.

In Hanford, eighty or more years ago, I knew often what "blind drunk" meant because my father was not averse to getting me drunk at a very early age. I was not quite eight years old when he first got me drunk and I believe that I almost died because he had no idea how potent his home brew was, especially inside a young boy. I remember he stuck his finger down my throat and made me vomit two or three times. He made me swallow a raw egg, too, and I think today that I *remember* what vomiting was like; I remember that it was one of the processes of life, and so I miss it.

On the inside of my right arm, barely an inch below my elbow, I have a penny-sized scar. I cannot see the scar now because the rat is on the floor near the chair and his gaze is out the window, but I *could* see the scar if I wanted to. It's a scar my father gave me once when he was drunk and I was very young. He came to my bed quite early one winter morning and whispered, "Gonna teach you about pain, Elmo." Then he held the lighted end of his cigar to the spot where that scar is now. I flinched, certainly, but I didn't draw my arm back because I was so damned surprised that my own father would do that to me. He never did anything like it again. It was, in fact, the only overtly cruel thing he ever did to me.

I like that scar. It's something real, it's something I can touch. My past is in it.

Jeff found his way into the library. He made his own cocoa, in fact, and some for me, and we sat in our usual chairs.

"You have to tell me why you carry that rat around with you, Elmo," he said, nodding at the wicker basket. "Is it a pet?" He grinned; it made the rat uneasy.

"Yes," I answered. "There are so few dogs left—"

"None, really," Jeff cut in. "I killed them all." Another grin, and again the rat became uneasy. "I killed several cats, too. Not all of them, of course, because they eat the rats."

I nodded. "That's very clear-headed of you, Jeff."

He nodded. "It is, isn't it? God, Elmo, I'm thinking *very* clearly these past few days. It surprises me how clearly I've been thinking."

"Good, Jeff," I managed. "Good. I'm glad."

"You're mumbling, Elmo. You sound like you've put marbles in your mouth. It's all I can do to carry on a normal conversation with you. And if I can't carry on a conversation with *you*, who else is there? I've killed all the survivalists." A brief pause. "So please get the marbles out of your mouth, Elmo."

"I'm sorry," I said.

"That's better." Another pause. "I want to tell you something." He sipped his cocoa. "You make this better than I do. You should drink some of it—*drink* some of it, Elmo."

I lifted the cup of cocoa to my lips, pretended to drink. I explained, "I really don't like cocoa, Jeff—"

He interrupted. "Did you notice that I've grown?"

I started to speak; he interrupted, "An inch, at least. I can't explain it, I don't want to explain it, I only know that I really feel *great*, Elmo! I feel *powerful*, very powerful!" A short pause. "Elmo, have you ever been to a party, a raucous party, a loud and raucous party, and when you got there you had been saying to yourself again and again, 'I'm not going to have any fun here, those people are too loud and raucous,' but after you were there an hour or so you began to feel . . . infected by it, and something inside you—your inhibitions, Elmo—started slipping away, and maybe an hour later you were just as loud and raucous as everyone else?"

"Certainly," I said.

"Certainly," he said, and grinned again. "The world just had a party, Elmo. It had its last big fling, and I am feeling so *good* because of it, so *good*. You look awful, Elmo. Is something wrong?"

"Just tired, Jeff."

"I can imagine. Look at me, please."

"I am."

"Over here, Elmo." He snapped his fingers. "Over here. That's right. Got to go now, nice talking to you, hope we'll talk again real soon—that is if you're not planning on going somewhere. Are you?"

"I don't know. I don't think so, Jeff."

"Of course you aren't," he said and grinned. The rat peed.

Jeff left.

I want to talk about my first kill.

I need to talk about my first kill. Call it nostalgia, I suppose.

My memory of it stirs something sweet in me.

Bitter-sweet. I could never taste blood, though I've always wanted to.

My first kill was a young boy named George who lived two miles from our house on Phillips Road and I remember he was coming home late from school—he was a good boy who did what he was told and he'd been told to stay late and clean the blackboards—and I swept over him with my arms wide and I remember he turned around and began to laugh at me. He thought it was a joke, poor little bastard.

Then I killed him.

And I threw his body into a culvert by the road. I heard his little head go *Sploosh!* into a rock, and I'm happy now that I didn't look.

My rat died and I have found a cat to take its place. I've given the cat a name. I have named it Leland Bohannon.

I heard something today as I slept. I heard someone singing, a woman singing, as if she were calling to me from a great distance. It was an extraordinarily beautiful sound that lasted a good minute or more, and I guessed that its direction from me was up. Not straight up, but obliquely up. And when I looked, as I slept, I saw only the dim suggestion of her. She had her arms extended to me.

Then her singing ended abruptly and she was gone, as if someone had closed a heavy door between us to keep us apart.

27

——

The cat has a much wider field of view than the rat. It also has a more highly developed color sense (I'm not sure that the rat saw in color at all) and I find that as I watch the pink first light of morning I have no compulsion at all to go into my cellar.

I'm not sure that what happened to Lewis Perdue so long ago wouldn't happen to me. We are two unique creatures, he with his strengths and weaknesses, and I with mine. I know that I could walk naked in the sunlight for whole minutes at a time without harm, and I know that I could stay here in this chair and watch the morning come through the eyes of the cat, and I would be no worse for it.

"We're going on a trip, Elmo," Jeff said.

"A trip, Jeff? To where?"

"No, no, Elmo, not 'To where?' *Why?* What *kind* of trip?"

He was standing on Tad Hamilton's front steps. He had his can of gasoline in hand again, and his matches.

It was not quite dusk, but the sky was dark from a low overcast. A light rain was falling.

Jeff continued, "We're going on a voyage of discovery, Elmo. Think of it, think of what's *out* there, beyond this grimy little village, now—after the war. All *hell* has broken loose on the world, Elmo, and it is up to us to make the most of it."

"I prefer staying here, Jeff, in this house."

He shook his head. "You can't do that, Elmo. Sorry. I'm going to burn this house."

"I wish you wouldn't."

"Your wishes are of no concern to me, my friend." He started down the steps, stopped, looked back. "We'll be leaving at seven-thirty tomorrow morning. Be ready."

He *is* taller. Louder, too. And wider—not obese, but very powerful-looking. He is not the same creature who called to me from across the village square several months ago.

Nor am I the same creature he called to.

A plague of grasshoppers tonight. They came in through cracks in the house and threw themselves against the screen at the front of the wicker basket that I keep the cat in. Then they swarmed over me. They're gone now, and the cat is slowly recovering.

"I'm awfully sorry, Elmo," Jeff said. He nodded at the wicker basket. "But you can't bring that."

"I need to bring it, Jeff."

"Oh? Why?"

"It's my pet."

"Is it litter-trained?" He grinned. Each of his grins seems more intensely malicious than the last. "Is it going to shit all over everything? We can't have *that*, can we?"

"I'll clean up after it. I promise."

He threw his big head back and his mane of blond hair pointed straight down. He opened his mouth wide, laughed. And when he was done laughing, he said, "You do that, Elmo." He laughed again. Then he went on, "I found a van, one without windows in the back—perfect for you, huh?"

"I don't understand," I said.

"Sure you do, Elmo." He looked at the wicker basket. "Mee-oow!" he said. "Sure you do," he repeated. "I'll go get the van now. You *will* be ready, won't you?"

"Yes."

"Good. I wouldn't want to torch you along with this house."

We do not dream. We can't. This thing called a brain inside our skulls is nothing more than a liquified mass of dead tissue. No current passes through it. It might as well be water. In sleep we are freed, we become a part of existence—we have no hunger, or memory, or need. We *become* all that *is*. We experience nothing. We experience all. We are the sow bug underfoot, the stalk of wheat falling to the farmer's blade, the infant routing at its mother's breast, the stack of cumulus that some small boy makes monsters of, a summer leaf, the nose of a poet, mother of pearl.

It's not pleasant or unpleasant. And it is the very best place to be while Tad Hamilton's house is burning.

PART TWO

Jeff's Coming-out Party

28

He drives the way Lemuel used to, as if there is no other traffic on the road, and now, of course, there isn't. But I yelled to him anyway, "You seem to be going awfully fast, Jeff," because I suddenly felt extremely vulnerable, as if, should my bones indeed snap it would bring me intense pain.

He yelled back, "I'm in charge here, Elmo. You just do . . . whatever it is that you do."

"I don't understand," I said.

"Sure you do," he said.

He had laid down a mattress for me in the back of the van, which was something he didn't need to do because it makes no difference to me where I sleep, but I saw it as a small act of compassion.

The last time I performed some small act of compassion, I remember, was in Hanford, eighty years ago, several days before I met Regina Watson. I took a wounded chipmunk out of the middle of Phillips Road and put it in tall grass along the shoulder. It probably died right away. It was pretty badly torn up, as if a cat had gotten at it, had had its way with it for a while, then let it go. So maybe it wasn't an act of compassion at all, maybe the most compassionate thing I could have done for it was put my boot to it and end its suffering.

Jeff said, "You know something, Elmo? You really are getting smaller. Are you eating right?"

"I'm on a fast," I told him.

"Oh, some kind of religious thing?"

"Yes. I'm very religious. I go on regular fasts—it's a cleansing experience—"

"So I've heard."

We were well away from Mumford at the time, a good twenty-five miles, I'd guess, and along the way I was able, fleetingly, to see through the eyes of half a dozen people, at least, who were watching us.

They were watching from various places—from houses and from hillsides, one was watching from his car, which he had pulled off the road and shut off when he'd heard the van. And I think it's interesting indeed that I had no trouble at all reading these people, most of them anyway (a few were just as opaque as Jeff), and I believe that if my heart still worked it would actually have quickened slightly.

"You look like you're kind of shrivelling up, Elmo!" Jeff called from the driver's seat. "You really should eat. Why don't I see if I can find a supermarket or something? I'm famished!"

"Yes," I answered, "that would be good." Then,

taking a chance, I added, "Jeff, do you know that we're being watched?"

And he answered quickly, "Sure I know it. You think I give a damn? You think they can touch me, Elmo? *No one* can touch me. Not them, not you, not anyone!"

Death is the glue that kept Jack Nelson's house together. It keeps me together, too. I see myself through Leland Bohannon's eyes, and I see what Jeff sees. I see a twenty-year-old man whom age caught up with almost eighty years ago and who has been pushing his own corruption back ever since through the murder of others. It is a face that is a mask. It does not breathe or animate. It merely exists, and even the cat will not focus on the eyes because it sees no eyes. It sees what try to pass for eyes, like the markings on the wings of a butterfly, and it is not fooled.

"The world just had a party, Elmo," Jeff told me again. "And the party's over, everyone's gone home to bed. Everyone but me, and I'm *pumped*! Damn, I'm pumped! Aren't you pumped, Elmo?" He laughed. It was a hysterical laugh, and on anyone else it would have been the laugh of a madman, but on him it was clearly the laugh of a man who has lots of power, and knows it.

Jeff is no longer confused. He used to be, when I first met him. He did many things without reason. But now everything he does has reason to it, and purpose. I have no idea what purpose. He's opaque. He's like Lewis Perdue was, and Regina Watson, and Lemuel, too, at the last.

29

_____

I can read him again, I can see through his eyes, hear
through his ears, touch through him.

But he wants me to, he's *allowing* it. I hear this in
his head: "Hi, Elmo, you old fart! Come on in and set
a spell," and I know it's my dignity he wants.

I prefer seeing through the eyes of the cat.

I prefer being alone.

In the past eighty years I've grown used to it. I've
grown used to being inside myself.

And that's where Jeff is now. Inside me.

I prefer seeing through the eyes of the cat, but Jeff
said, "I thought we were friends, Elmo," and I shook
my head.

"I'm a friend to no one," I told him.

"That's very noble, I'm sure," he said, then laughed
deeply, and long, far too long for the remark he'd
made. When he stopped he said, "It's daylight, Elmo.

Can't you see that it's daylight? I thought you worked the night-shift," and he laughed yet again, just as deeply and just as long. He got so involved in it, in fact, that he went off the road and into a ditch.

I found myself lying face down on the right wall of the van. The wicker basket, with Leland Bohannon in it, was on top of me. I saw all this through Jeff's eyes. He was making his way out of the driver's seat and back to me, still laughing, though not quite so deeply—I think there might even have been some pain in it.

He lay down on his stomach next to me. I turned my head very shakily, much as an infant will, as if to look at him. He let me see him, then, through Leland Bohannon's eyes, and I saw that he was smiling coyly, as if at a private joke, and that he was propping himself up on his elbows, and had his eyes on me.

He said, "We're a pair, aren't we, Elmo? Heckel and Jeckell, Jekyll and Hyde, Hyde and Hyde. We really are a pair!"

I said, "Jeff, I don't know you anymore."

He answered, "You never did, old sport. But I'm only what you are, I'm only a man who's interested in survival, just someone who wants to live to fight another day." He turned his head so his gaze was on his hands lying flat in front of him. "Don't feel sorry for yourself, Elmo. You had your turn, now it's mine." He thought a moment, grinned, added, "Ours."

"Ours?" I asked.

"Yes." He rolled away from me and crawled out through the rear doors of the van. "I'll push it back," he called. "Hang on." And seconds later I was on my back on the bed of the van; the wicker basket was near the driver's seat. And since I was seeing through Leland Bohannon's eyes, the view I got was of the back of the seat, and something of the driver's door. Jeff got in and started the van. Soon we were moving again, and again I was seeing through his eyes. Seeing, at the horizon, what looked like the remains of a city, as if some gigantic child had thrown a tantrum in it and kicked it apart. A bluish haze was over it, like smog, and here and there an occasional, brief glint of fire.

Jeff said, "That's *my* kind of place."

The engine started acting up. Within a few minutes it died. Jeff cursed hotly—"Did'joo do that, Elmo?" he called, and laughed again. He threw open his door, went around to the back, opened the rear doors. "How you doin' there, sport?" he asked. I was not doing well.

I told him, barely at a whisper, "The light bothers me, Jeff."

"'Course it does," he said. "But we gotta move on. We got places to go, people to see!"

I hissed at him. I have done quite a lot of hissing in the last eighty years. It comes naturally. And it is, naturally, a very threatening gesture.

"Don't do that," Jeff said, annoyed. "Christ almighty, you don't know how much you stink, Elmo." And he threw the doors shut.

My very first kill was a boy named Georgie who was late coming home from school because he'd stayed after to clean the blackboards. He was a good boy. I knew him. Not well, but in passing. He had come to my father's house several times hoping our hen had laid a few extra eggs, and when she had he went home happy.

His house was two miles from my father's house. It was a very large and very ramshackle Victorian farmhouse, and Georgie lived there with his two brothers, four sisters, his mother and father, and assorted animals. That family was the epitome of "dirt poor", but Georgie's mother managed somehow to dress him halfway decently for school. Indeed, she took great pride in the fact that he *could* go to school—he was the only one of the children who was allowed to, in fact, because he was the brightest.

And when he turned and saw me sweeping toward him that evening he said, "Hey, Elmo, how ya doin?'" and the thought passed through his head that he wanted to tell me about something he'd learned at school that day. But that's when I tore him up and threw him into the culvert.

He'd be dead now, anyway. Like everyone else.

Like Lemuel, like Regina Watson, and Lewis Perdue, like that pretty young thing he pointed out to me from the restaurant. Like my mother and my father.

Maybe they're all better off.

"Can you feel it, Elmo?" Jeff said. He had thrown open the rear doors of the van and was holding them open with his hands. He was very excited.

"Feel what?" I asked. It was evening. Behind him I could see the Big Dipper near the northern horizon. I looked at it for a few seconds. I remembered that in Hanford, eighty years ago, I had found it somehow comforting. It comforted me now.

"*Something* in the *air*," Jeff said. I was seeing him through the eyes of the cat. "Something . . ." He paused, then went on at a whisper, "Something powerful!" He looked straight into Leland Bohannon's eyes.

"Yes, Elmo. Something powerful," he said, still at a whisper, but a whisper that was tight and certain.

He continued, "It's night, Elmo," and stepped to one side so I could get out. "And we're going to do some walking." He grinned. "I can carry you if you're not up to it."

"I'm up to it," I said testily.

Leland Bohannon has superb night vision. His hearing is excellent, too, and he's very alert. He twitches and grows excited and tense with every movement in the tall grasses at the shoulder of the road. I have him trussed up with thin twine inside the wicker basket, and now and then I reach in and stroke him to keep him contented. I know from the cat himself if I'm stroking him in the right way, and it has taken me no small amount of practise to get the movement of my hand and fingers correct, very much as if I'm operating some kind of robot arm and trying to pick up something delicate with it.

I have developed a certain . . . feeling for the cat, the same kind of feeling, probably, that a living man

241

has for his eyes and ears and fingers, because they are his connection to the real world.

Jeff said, "You keep a very uneven pace, Elmo. You walk as if your knees are bolted shut." He laughed shortly. "Why do you walk like that?"

"Arthritis," I told him.

"Uh-huh," he said, "and I'm the Queen of France."

We were on a narrow dirt road that branched off the main road. To the left I could see a thin and badly rusted wire connecting old wooden fence posts, and I could hear a little brook moving along. Off to the right, in what appeared to be acres and acres of tall grass, a fox was following us. It looked up every few steps, and for moments at a time I saw myself through its eyes. I thought I looked very much like Ratzo Rizzo tripping along that road.

I was again wearing a polo shirt, Nike tennis shoes, a pair of blue Bermuda shorts.

"You don't have arthritis at all, I'll bet," Jeff said.

"You'd win the bet," I said.

I felt a very light touch at my shoulders. He had put his arm there, around my shoulders. "I like you, Elmo." His tone was very warm and friendly. "You're all right. Screwed up, sure, but you're all right." He paused for thought, then went on, "We're a pair, aren't we? Hekyll and Jekyll, Hyde and Hyde." He laughed. "Get it, Elmo? Hyde and Hyde? Get it?"

"No," I said, "explain it to me."

He took his arm away and stopped walking. I stopped. Leland Bohannon was close to panicking in his efforts to find the fox again, so the view I was getting of Jeff was quickly on again and off again.

Jeff said, "Yes, I think that you do understand and I think you're lying to me. That's not a good basis for a friendship, Elmo. We are among the last survivors of the last great war. We *have* to be friends." He put his arm around my shoulder again and whispered conspiratorially, "I know everything there is to know about you, Elmo, and I'll keep your little secret. Really." He let go of my shoulder. He nodded at the wicker basket, "I'll even let you keep the little kitty cat, if you'd like. Just as long as you . . ." He thought for a moment, continued, "As long as you do this *thing* with me, Elmo."

"What thing?"

"The kind of thing you've *always* done! Don't play the fool, Elmo, it doesn't fit you." He was upset, and beginning to talk loudly. "The kind of thing you've been doing for eighty years, goddammit—don't tell me you've forgotten how—"

"I don't need to do it anymore, Jeff."

"Of course you do." He started walking again. The fox started walking again; the cat's eyes levelled on it. "Look at you. You're shrivelling up. You look like a goddamn prune, for Christ's sake. *I* know what you need just as well as you do—"

"I'm dying, Jeff."

He laughed another of his long, maniacal laughs. And when he was done he grabbed the wicker basket from me, held it up to his face and said to Leland Bohannon, and so to me, "You asshole, you friggin' asshole, how can you be dying if you're already dead?"

30

"And I'm alive, Elmo. I can touch, I can hear, I can see. Even through the soles of my shoes I know that the road is covered with little stones. I know that wood is burning somewhere close by, because I can smell it. I can smell you, too, and that cat—you should clean up after it, Elmo; let it out to take a crap every now and then, okay?

"And I can smell wet grass, too—so I know it must have rained recently.

"So you see, Elmo, even in the dark I'm still in touch with the earth. But you aren't. You're in touch with Elmo Land. You've got your finger on your own non-existent pulse, and I'll bet you don't like it much, do you?"

"No, I don't," I said.

"Thanks for your honesty. I like honesty. I hope you'll always be honest with me."

"I could tear you apart, Jeff," I growled.

And he said, "Sorry, Elmo, I didn't hear you— you're going to *have* to speak up."

I said nothing.

He has found a place for us to stay, a big red house with white shutters, a full basement, a finished attic, and a fieldstone patio with a large, home-made barbecue. There's a rec room with a pool table and video games in the basement, and right off the rec room is a big, dark room that was once used as a storage area, Jeff says.

I asked him, "Did you live here?" And he said no, he never lived here, it was just a house he liked the look of, that the people who used to live in it were his kind of people.

"You knew them?" I asked.

He shook his head.

"Then how do you know what kind of people they were?"

He gave me one of the starkly malicious grins that make Leland Bohannon very nervous. "I'm smart, I guess," he said, and made it clear from his tone that the subject was at an end.

An hour before sunrise he made something for us that looked like a hamburger. He cooked it on the home-made barbecue, served it on some blue Wedgwood plates he found in a big, oak hutch in the dining room, and told me, "Let's eat up, Elmo." He grinned broadly, as if he had said something very funny.

There is a black, wrought-iron table on the patio,

with matching chairs, and a big, white umbrella with the word *Smirnoff* on it in green.

We were seated at the table. The wicker basket, with Leland Bohannon in it, was to my left on the table-top; it was aimed at Jeff. I said to him, "I'm not very hungry."

"You'll like this," he said.

"What is it?"

"What is it?" He paused; he grinned again. "It's . . . rabbit." Another pause. "Yeah. It's rabbit, Elmo."

"I've never liked rabbit," I said. It was true. I grew tired of rabbit eighty years ago because we had it at least three times a week. It was always served the same way, roasted, with white potatoes, an occasional green vegetable, and well water to drink. "I can't eat it," I said to Jeff. "It makes me ill."

"Uh-huh." He stuck his fork into it, sawed off a small piece with a steak knife, studied the piece for quite a while, and popped it into his mouth. "Lots of things make you ill, don't they, Elmo? Why is that?"

"I've always been ill."

"Always?"

"Always. Yes. Ever since I was an infant."

He sawed off another piece of the rabbit, studied it, popped it into his mouth, chewed for quite some time. "You were an infant? I find that hard to believe. You look like an infant now, all wrinkled up and small." He grinned.

I sensed hunger from Leland Bohannon. I said to Jeff, "Can the cat have a piece of that?" I nodded at Jeff's plate.

He shrugged. "Sure. Feed him yourself, Elmo." His

lips quivered into a half-grin. "If you're not hungry," he continued. So I put the piece of rabbit that Jeff had given me into the wicker basket with the cat, who started devouring it immediately.

Jeff said, "You should feed him more often; my God, he's beginning to look as bad as you do." Then he put the last bit of rabbit into his mouth, chewed it for quite some time, as if the meat were tough, swallowed, and pushed himself away from the table. "Good day, Elmo," he said, stood, and wandered off into the early morning darkness. I stayed where I was and watched the first few minutes of daylight come.

I went inside.

We both sleep in the cellar, Jeff in a far corner of the room on a folding cot he found in a closet upstairs, and I in the storage area, with Leland Bohannon, in another corner far from Jeff, on the floor.

Little Luke, Regina Watson's boy, looked just like a plump, over-stuffed, white nylon doll whose mouth has been made from two folds of its own nylon skin stitched tightly together, whose eyes are fashioned from tiny bright blue buttons, and whose nose seems very much an afterthought because half of it is missing and the half is ragged and fraying at the edges.

It's nearly the way that I looked for quite some time after my transformation—pale, but plump, because food was plentiful. I don't think I look that way anymore. I don't really have a good idea *what* I look

247

like. I rely on Jeff for that. And perhaps someday I'll turn the wicker basket in my direction and see what Leland Bohannon sees.

I heard something today as I slept. I heard a woman singing, as if she were calling to me from a great distance. It was an extraordinarily beautiful sound, and it lasted a good ten minutes or more. Its direction, I guessed, was up. Not straight up, but obliquely up. And when I looked, as I slept, I saw the dim suggestion of her. She had her arms extended, a welcoming smile was on her lips, and for a moment she interrupted her singing to say my name once, and again.

Then she was gone.

31

This house has ghosts in it. They are the ghosts of the children who used to live here and during the day they peek into the storage area where I sleep. They giggle and ask each other who I am and what I'm doing here. I try to speak to them because they wake me, but they won't hear me. I don't know why. I want them to hear me. I want to apologize to them because they are children, and little Georgie might as well have been one of them. *I* am one of them. I would dearly love to be out there, giggling with them, waiting to be called away. As all the dead in Mumford were.

It has become increasingly difficult for me to get around. Through Leland Bohannon's eyes it's clear that I lurch this way and that, like a drunk, and Jeff says to me at such times, "Hey, hold on to something, Elmo, old sport; you're falling apart," and laughs, or he tells me my knees are bolted together, or he offers to carry me. It would be good to be in touch with myself again, good to feel my feet hitting the earth, good to be *aware* of my body. But that's behind me, and walking is now purely a matter of trial and error, hit and miss. So I fall down quite a lot. Jeff usually lets me lie where I've fallen, sometimes for quite a while, I think, with Leland Bohannon—who has taken to meowing most of the time; I believe that he's dying—pointed away from me. That's when I let the memories crowd back. I love them. *I'm* in them, Mrs Land's baby boy, brought into the world at home on a bright April day in 1907, pink as a spring sunrise, plopped into a basinette, thanks given, a new life for the world.

Here I am. Inside this creature. Inside this old corpse that still attempts to walk about. Here I am, somewhere behind the medulla oblongata, crying my eyes out, like a three-year-old.

And I did so love the things I had to do because that's when the need ended, and peace came, and the baby slept.

But now I'm being sung to, and seduced. I'm able to chase the hunger away.

Rabbit again. "I love rabbit," Jeff told me. "I used to shoot rabbits when I was a boy. I shot them with arrows, and bb guns, and with a Twenty-two when I was old enough—I dearly loved to shoot them. Now they're everywhere. I don't know why. Have you seen them?"

"No, I haven't seen any rabbits," I said.

He grinned. "Of course you haven't." He took the piece of rabbit he'd been cooking at the barbecue, which is a couple yards away from the patio set, and brought it back to the table. It was a piece about as big as a man's hand. "Big rabbit," he said. He was holding it up on his barbecue fork, in front of his eyes. "Some for you, Elmo?"

"No," I said.

"You don't mind if I pig out, do you?" He sat down across from me and put the rabbit on his plate.

"I don't mind," I said.

He sawed off a small piece, studied it, put it into his mouth. He said while he chewed, "*Good* rabbit." He swallowed, grinned. "Hop-hop," he said. "You *are* what you *eat*." He took another bite, chewed once, twice, spat it out. "Goddamn tough little bastard!"

I said to him, because something strange had passed between his brain and mine, if only for a moment, "That's not rabbit at all, is it, Jeff?"

Another grin. Another piece of the rabbit went into his mouth. He said as he chewed, "You've got to trust me, Elmo."

The sun started rising then. He glanced at it, stuffed the rest of the rabbit into his shirt pocket—"For later," he explained—and went into the house, down to the cellar, to sleep.

Jeff says we're near a town called Geneva. He tells me it was once a college town, but that the college is gone now, someone burned it, he says. I asked him if he burned it. He said no, someone else burned it. The war burned it. He said he's just picking up where the war left off.

He asked me again, "Have you ever been to a really loud and raucous party, Elmo? And when you got there you said to yourself, 'I'm not going to have any fun here, these people are too loud and raucous.' But after a while you found that you were having a little fun, that you were getting into the *spirit* of things, so to speak, and when the party ended you were really *pumped*. Well, I'm pumped, I'm damn pumped—the world just had a party, and I'm *pumped*!"

Then he told me that there were people living in the town.

"People?" I said.

He nodded. We were sitting at the patio set, it was a little past midnight. He nodded again, to his right: "If you look, you can see some lights burning, Elmo. They've got electric power from somewhere. I don't know from where, but I'll find out. They've even got a radio station going—they're playing Top Forty stuff."

I turned my head in the direction he'd indicated. The cat's head stayed still, its eyes on Jeff, so I could see nothing of the town.

"They're all assholes," Jeff went on. He's taken up smoking. He had a pack of Tareytons in his pocket. He took it out, shook it so one of the filter tips appeared, put the cigarette between his lips. "They're talking about bringing civilization back." He grinned and shook his head as if at a distasteful joke. "A bunch of assholes, a bunch of bubble-heads, Elmo. They're even drawing up something they call a Town Constitution." He shook his head again, more briskly, as if in anger. "There's hardly a sane head in the whole bunch, Elmo."

I asked, "What are you going to do to them?"

He answered, "I'm going to burn them."

"Yes. I thought so," I said.

He said, "Speak up, Elmo. Christ, you're getting harder and harder to understand these days. You're falling apart."

"Just tired," I said.

"No," he said. "Obsolete."

I saw Regina Watson once after my transformation. It was early Christmas morning, 1928, and for the first time in almost half a century snow had come to Hanford, Kentucky. Not much, two inches perhaps, and it was doubtless gone by midday. But to my eyes, even then, a year after my transformation, it was very pleasant. I remember standing near the house on Phillips Road, just inside a stand of piney woods, and watching it collect on rooftops and chimneys and on my father's Buick. I had never, in life, seen anything like that snow. Christmas at the Land household was always a green and humid affair. We never had a tree, only an occasional wreath that my mother fashioned from small branches she'd gathered in the piney woods.

And as I watched the snow piling up, from those same woods, that Christmas, 1928, I sensed something graceful moving toward me through the darkness, some night creature prowling because of hunger, and confused by the snow.

Then I felt my father get out of his bed, because of the cold, go to a window, and look out. I saw through his eyes the wide, graceful flakes piling up every-where, moving in the darkness like moths, not quite getting all the way down into the piney woods, turning the tree-tops white.

"Myrna," my father called, "come see this here." But she was asleep.

I felt him smile. I felt his pleasure at the snow. I saw his eyes linger on me for several seconds.

"Myrna," he called again, "come here." But she stayed asleep. He continued to watch the snow collect. He said to himself that he didn't remember that stump being there, at the front of the piney woods, because he didn't know, of course, that the stump was his son. His son was buried somewhere in Regina Watson's house. God knew where.

Then his gaze settled on other things—on his Buick, on his own reflection from the window, on the snow again. On me. He saw Regina Watson come up behind me through the woods. He saw her put her arms around me. Then he looked at the snow again and he thought it was beautiful. He hoped it would last through Christmas Day.

I wish I could call to him now. Back eighty years; "Hey, it's me, Elmo, your son, and I've come back. Do you still love me?"

But I can call to no one. I'm like a termite eating someone's house up. I can't be talked to or reasoned with, I can only be exterminated. And now the house has fallen down around me and has turned to dust.

There is no work left for me to do.

32

___

Leland Bohannon died. I woke, he was purring, his eyes half open, his gaze on Jeff, who was across the room, his body just barely outlined by light filtering in from the rest of the cellar. And I felt Leland Bohannon's heartbeat begin to stop. It is normally very fast, but as I listened, and by slow degrees, it came to a halt. Leland Bohannon went on purring for several seconds, his eyes went on seeing, and he began to turn his head as if to look at me. He got as far as my forehead. I saw little through his eyes, only what looked for all the world like a flat, dead fish. Then his head slumped forward and he was dead.

I became blind then, and deaf. The storage area is strangely free of insects or rodents and the only other creature whose senses I could have used was Jeff, who was asleep.

"Your cat died, Elmo," Jeff said. I could see him above me. He had his hands on his hips and had taken his shirt off. He looked very muscular, like Arnold

Schwarzenegger, and it's not the way I first saw him. He's taller, and he's louder, too. He went on, grinning, "And I got rid of it for you—no, don't thank me. I didn't want it stinking the place up—you do that well enough all by yourself. Gawd, Elmo, take a *bath*!" His grin broadened. He continued, "Anyway, I got you another pet, one more suited to you, I think. I got you a little fruit bat. They're everywhere, now, like the rabbits. It's all tied up in that basket of yours. No, don't thank me. I know you're an animal lover. I gave the cat a good, Christian burial, too. Like I did the people in Mumford. Did you have a name for it?"

"Yes."

"Speak up, Elmo. You're mumbling again."

"Yes, I had a name for it. Its name was Leland Bohannon."

He laughed quickly. "Elmo, that's a stupid name for a cat." Then he went to the door of the storage area and opened it. I could see the hint of daylight beyond coming in through the cellar windows. He turned his head, looked at the wicker basket, into the bat's eyes, at me. "I'm working the day-shift, Elmo," he said, and added, "I'll see you later."

I do not dream. I can't. This thing called a brain inside my skull is nothing more, I think, than a liquified mass of dead tissue. No electricity passes through it. It might as well be water.

But in sleep I am free. I become a part of all that is. I have no hunger, I have no memory, I have no need. I *become* all that *is*. I am the sow bug underfoot, the stalk of wheat that falls to the farmer's blade, the infant routing at its mother's breast, the stack of cumulus that some small boy makes monsters of, a summer leaf, the nose of a poet, mother of pearl.

I am all my victims. I am little Georgie, I am frightened, red-haired Orry.

Lemuel told me, in 1959, strutting about in his thirty-dollar Sears three-piece suit, in the house in Dundotton, Maryland, "I don't need you no more. Damn, Elmo, I'm closin' in on bein' *fifty* years old and what I got to show for bein' that old? I got a long line of dead people behind me callin' my name, tellin' me how worthless I am, that I ain't got no future."

And I see them, now. I see a line of the dead that hasn't moved in eighty years. No one sings to them, and no one calls to them. Their souls float inside them like dead fish in a bowl.

Once, I was going to be a minister. I was going to do some bible thumping and some preaching and I was going to save lots of souls. That was when I was twelve or thirteen, when people first get religion. I was going to be a Baptist minister because they seemed to *believe* so much more strongly than any other kind of minister. They were *certain* of everything—they were certain of their goodness and certain of their evil.

So I went into the Hanford First Baptist Church when I thought it was empty—a winter night in 1920 when everyone should have been home trying to keep the cold damp out of their houses—and I gave a sermon. It was one hell of a sermon. It said, in essence, that God had put us on the earth for one reason only, and that was to tell him how thankful we were to Him for doing it. And when I was done, someone stepped out of the shadows at the back of the church just enough that I could see he was there, and he said, "You sure are an ignorant little bastard, Elmo Land." Then he laughed a long, maniacal laugh. (Jeff laughs that way.) Then he turned and left, but not before I saw that it was Herbert Lincoln, whom everyone in Hanford thought quite a lot of. Five years later he killed his wife and children with a twelve gauge shotgun. Then he came to my father's house and turned the weapon on me. "You're gonna die, anyway, you ignorant little bastard!" he said, and pulled the trigger. The gun was empty. My father came out and chased him away with a hatchet.

Lemuel told me, as well, in the little house in Dundotton, "I may be stupid, Elmo. Shit, I *know* how stupid I am, but I gotta tell you this, I ain't insane, I ain't crazy, I ain't got no toys in my attic. I'm jus' lots stronger than you. Shit, you had to go and die to get to likin' the taste of blood—you had to go and *die* to like it, so fuck you and fuck Regina and fuck Jack Nelson and fuck Lewis Perdue! I'm gonna go sell some cars."

He would have dearly loved this war. Just as Jeff did.

I'm like a termite eating someone's house up. I can't be reasoned with, only destroyed, and the house has turned to dust around me.

33

"They're sure tough little bastards, Elmo," Jeff said to me this evening, on the patio, both of us seated at the patio set. He did not eat, tonight. He said something about having eaten earlier. "I mean," he went on expansively, and a look of happy reflection came into his eyes, "you *think* they're gonna go just like that"— he snapped his fingers—"because they look so small, and so weak (I guess the war did that), but they hang on. Jesus, you have to hand it to them, Elmo. You have to hand it to them."

I asked, "What are you talking about?"

"About those slobs in town, of course," he answered.

"I don't understand."

"Sure, you do. I've been *killing* them. And it's really in a good cause because the weak ones wouldn't last the winter, anyway. I'm doing us all a favor. We all have to eat, we all have to survive." He had turned his head and was looking directly into the wicker basket, and so at me. He went on, less expansively, as if getting onto a lighter subject, "So what did *you* do today, Elmo?"

"Nothing," I answered. "What can I do?"

He shrugged. "That's a good question." He gave me a flat smile. "Hell, you can *rot*, Elmo." He nodded toward the town. "Like them. You can rot." He moved his gaze up and down the front of the wicker basket, as if giving me the once-over. "Have you seen yourself lately?" he asked.

"No," I said. "I haven't."

"Because you really do look awful. You look like you're falling apart."

"Yes," I said, "you've told me that before."

"And it's getting truer every day, Elmo." He sat back in his chair and put his hands behind his head, as if he had suddenly gotten into a reflective mood. "Do you believe in evil?"

"Yes," I answered. "I do."

He shook his head. "You're wrong, then. There is no 'evil', there's *compulsion*. The war taught me that. It taught me about *their* compulsions"—another nod toward the town—"and it taught me about my own."

Dimly, I was aware that we'd had a similar conversation some time ago, but I knew that it was not quite the same this time, that roles had been traded, somehow.

A woman appeared.

"Hi," she said. She was standing to Jeff's left, near the corner of the house. She was wearing a pleated skirt, a white blouse, and she was young, no more than twenty, I think, and her features were even, she was probably quite attractive. She was smiling, too, and she had a small handgun pointed at Jeff's head.

"Hi," Jeff said, his tone very cordial, as if he were

about to invite her to sit down with us, and as a matter of fact he nodded at the table, and gestured at it, but she fired before he could say anything more. The bullet hit him in the center of the chest. A small hole appeared there, and blood began vaulting out of him in time with his pulse almost at once.

He tore his shirt open, looked down at himself—he was clearly astonished—then collapsed face forward onto the patio table. The woman began to weep. She dropped her handgun, stared at Jeff for several seconds, and then, for the first time—it was well past dusk—her eyes appeared to settle on me. She stopped weeping. She whispered, deep in her throat, "For the love of God!"

"Hello," I said, and made as if to doff an invisible hat.

"For the love of God!" she said again, and fled.

This evening the ghosts of the children who lived in this house came up from the cellar to the patio set where Jeff and I are, gathered around us, giggled at us, whispered to each other. Then they went back to the cellar. They are creatures of compulsion, too.

Jeff moves occasionally. His hands twitch and his back flutters—his shirt flutters, actually, as if a breeze is moving it. Blood has pooled around his face, but because the little fruit bat he found for me does not see in color it doesn't look at all like blood, it looks like coffee, even with the light of early morning on it.

Toward the east, from the direction of the town, I have heard occasional gunfire and it makes me wonder if the young woman who shot Jeff did it out of revenge or merely because the world has lately been in a killing mood and she caught on to it.

As Lemuel did, so many years ago. "He was a tough little bastard, Elmo, real wiry," he said, "but he's all taken care of, all done, he used to be a friend of my daddy's, his name was Leland Bohannon. He and my daddy used to go fishin' together, and drinkin' together. Hell, Elmo, I guess he used to bounce me on his knee when I was an infant, though I don't remember that, of course, and he didn't recognize me, I guess. Oh, maybe a little, maybe I seen somethin' in those tiny brown eyes a his like he know'd who I was—"

I knew so well about compulsion. Here I am, inside this creature, this old corpse that still tries to animate itself, and I want to cry my eyes out.

I thank God I cannot live forever. I thank God that the house has fallen down around me and there is no more work for me to do.

34

"Make-up," Jeff said. "It covers a multitude of sins." He had his shirt apart. We were in the storage area, in the cellar, and he was standing near the door with daylight on him. "Make-up," he said again. "She winged me." He grinned. "She only winged me. Thank God." His grin broadened. He buttoned his shirt, then touched his forehead with his index finger. "She's crazy, they're *all* crazy. Stupid, too. Real stupid. To think she could come here, to *this* house, to our house, Elmo, and shoot me! Real stupid!"

The storage area door was halfway open. He pulled it all the way open and took a step out, paused. "I like the sunlight, I've always liked the sunlight. I tan well." He paused again, went on, "You don't, though. I'd say you don't tan at all well. I'd say you probably have a tendency to burn, isn't that right?"

"Yes," I said.

"Then this"—he nodded to indicate the dark storage area—"is the very best place for you." And he left.

*

On my tenth birthday, my father gave me a fishing pole he'd fashioned, quite expertly, from a length of birch. He had attached a new reel to it, and the reel had quite a bit of good, strong line on it.

I went fishing with that pole and reel that very day, even though it was raining ("Fish like to jump, Elmo, when it rains," my father said). I'd been fishing with my father a number of times before, of course, but I always had to fashion my own pole from whatever was available, and I always had to try and make do with six or seven feet of line attached to it.

My father didn't come with me that day. He didn't like to get wet. He had just a touch of arthritis and the dampness aggravated it. I went alone, to the same spot my father and I always went to—an acre-size spring-fed pond that had trout in it and an occasional Walleye—and I sat down close to the shore, in the same spot my father and I always sat down at. I cast some line out, badly, watched the rain pelt the water, and watched the fish jump—I was pleased my father was right about that—and I got very wet. I don't believe that I have ever enjoyed myself more.

"Rabbit," Jeff said. We were again at the patio set. He'd carried me there and had put me in my usual chair, with the wicker basket on the table, the opening pointed in his direction. He held the small piece of rabbit up on the end of his fork. "Rabbit," he repeated. "Lots of rabbits, lots of good eating, Elmo. Hop-hop"— he put the piece into his mouth—"you *are* what you *eat*! And I'll tell you something, Christ Lord in Heaven,

I'm famished, I could eat an army, I could eat *you*, Elmo." He grinned, longer and wider than the remark dictated. Then he went on, slicing another piece of rabbit from a large piece on his plate, "I found the woman that shot me and I slapped her around." He stuck the piece of rabbit into his mouth, chewed, went on as he chewed, "I really should have done more than that, I guess, but she's crazy. Hell, they're all crazy! And besides, maybe sometime I might want a little nooky, you know, and she's not too bad to look at." Another playful grin. He reached for me with his free hand, as if to poke my arm; "Better-looking than you, anyway, you old fart." He swallowed the piece of rabbit. "I found out her name, too," he continued, his tone casual now. "Her name's Melinda Becker and she used to be a dental assistant. Wasn't that what you were, Elmo?"

"No," I said.

"Sure you were, Christ your brain's turning to mush, Elmo."

"No, I was a pharmacist."

"You were a dental assistant, Elmo!" He was getting angry. "You were working on somebody when the war started—you *told* me that."

"It's not important."

"Of course it's important. My God, Elmo—this is my *memory* we're talking about here."

"Okay. I was a dental assistant. I was working on someone when the war started."

"Good." He smiled. He was pleased. "Just like Melinda Becker." He sliced another piece of rabbit for himself and popped it into his mouth. "Wouldn't I love to get a little bite of *her*! Christ, wouldn't I love that!" He chewed slowly, with great deliberation. "I could eat her up in two bites—that's lip-smacking good stuff there."

I said, "You were being worked on by a dentist when the war started. You told me it was a lady dentist."

He had something that looked like Coca-Cola in a yellowish plastic glass. He sipped at it, dribbled some of the stuff onto his chin, swiped at it with the back of his hand. "No, Elmo, I never told you that. Someone else must have told you that. It wasn't me." And he started eating some more of what he had told me was rabbit.

"Perhaps," I said.

"Because I"—he laboriously sliced a particularly tough piece of what he had told me was rabbit—"was on my way home, on the thruway, not more than fifty miles from here."

"Yes," I said.

"And I stopped at this thruway restaurant to eat and I heard someone say something about an explosion in St Louis."

"Yes," I said again.

He put his elbow on the table, held his fork straight up, a small piece of rabbit on it, and studied it as he talked. He smiled loosely, as if remembering something he'd been trying for a long time to remember. "And there was this guy—I remember now—there was this guy in the men's room who was sick—I remember now—and he asked could I please turn the light out."

I said nothing. He said nothing for a long while; only this, several times, smiling, "Hop-hop, Elmo. You *are* what you *eat*!"

When Regina Watson came to me that night, eighty years ago, the night after Lemuel and I saw her on the feather pillows in her kitchen, she did not float in, we cannot float—we are bound by most of the same physical laws that bind the living—she stepped in, over the window sill, her left leg first, then her right, her long, off-white dress hiked up to mid-thigh, and there was a waning gibbous moon that night which cast a cool, sultry glow on her. She looked hungry, and I could not see her eyes well because of the darkness in them, the shadow of her brow. I said to her, "Hi, Mrs Watson." She nodded. I saw the glint of her eyes, an off-white like the color of her dress, off-white and cool. Then she bent over me and said, "Hello, Mr Land," and she chuckled.

Minutes later, my father came in and saw her on my bed, the skinny black fingers of her hair caught in the orange glow of his kerosene lamp.

"Good boy, Elmo," my father said, certain that I had at last gotten rid of my cumbersome virginity.

It is the memory of my death and it moves around inside me now like something feverish and alone that has no place to put itself and no place to rest.

Jeff said, "Let me tell you about the people who used to live here." Again, we were at the patio set. Again

267

he had carried me there because I find it all but impossible to get around now. I feel something that might be pain when I try. And, as usual, the wicker basket was on the table, pointed at Jeff. It was early morning. To the north a low, ragged line of clouds had appeared. Overhead, the sky was crowded with stars. Jeff had set up a kerosene lamp near the patio set so it dangled from a length of rope he'd stretched between the house and the umbrella pole. Every once in a while a breeze moved it, pushing orange shadows across his face.

He seemed very animated, very amused. His wide, malicious grin came and went freely, and he smoked as he talked.

I asked, "You knew them?" It was a question, I remembered, that I'd asked once before.

"No." He looked momentarily confused. "But I can . . ."—he searched for the right word—"I can *feel* them," he went on. His grin altered a little, as if he were suddenly proud of himself. "I can *feel* them, Elmo. As if they're here, with me, at this table." His big, blond head turned to one side, his mouth dropped open slightly. He was in awe of himself. He turned his head quickly, looked straight into the wicker basket, and so at me. "Have *you* ever had feelings like that, Elmo?" He sounded desperate.

"Yes," I answered.

"And do you anymore?"

"No."

"Not at all?"

"Only sometimes."

He relaxed. He sat back in his patio chair, put his

hands behind his head and was quiet for several minutes, the orange glow of the kerosene lamp drifting this way and that across him in time with the early morning breeze. And at last he said, "They weren't very special. They were just people. They had sex parties, they drank too much, he liked Mantovanni. Big deal. A couple of slobs, like them"—he inclined his head briskly toward the town. "Like them," he repeated. Then he said, "Not like us, huh!"

"Us?"

"You and me, babe." He grinned. "We're a team, aren't we? Hekyll and Jekyll, Hyde and Hyde—Hyde in plain sight." He laughed quickly. "I know what you are, Elmo."

I said nothing.

"You're some kind of . . . mondo bizzaro, some kind of weirdo, maybe you're just a figment of my imagination."

"Maybe."

"I don't think so. I think you're as real as shit, Elmo, old sport." He leaned forward. He whispered into the wicker basket, "And can I tell you something else, Elmo?" He paused just a moment. "You *look* like shit! You're coming apart at the seams. Do you know, Elmo, that there are whole pieces of you missing." He laughed shortly.

"I wasn't aware of that," I said.

"And you sound like Vincent Price imitating Bela Lugosi."

I said nothing.

He leaned back suddenly. "Of course you're not

aware of it, Elmo. You're not even aware of your own gut, for Christ's sake."

"I'm aware of pain."

He leaned forward again, put his hands on the top of the table, folded them, looked very concerned. He said, "Are you? What kind of pain is it? You mean like a toothache?"

"No."

"You're drifting, Elmo, old sport, don't go away from me just now, I need you. What *kind* of pain?"

"I don't know."

"Of course you know. Of course you know! Asshole! *I* need to know—I don't *like* pain—"

"Who does?"

His hand swept across my face. I felt something like a quick, stiff wind passing. "*I* don't!" he said.

"Their pain," I said.

"Oh, for God's sake—"

"*Their* pain," I said again. "I have *their* pain, and I have my own pain, I have the world's pain—"

He threw his hands into the air in a gesture of disgust and frustration. "Christ, that's all I need, a fucking philosophical dead man!" He tossed his cigarette away, hurriedly lit another one, puffed on it as if in great agitation. "I *know* who you are, Elmo," he said once again.

"You seem nervous, Jeff."

He attempted a grin. "I know who you are," he said again. "And I don't *believe* in you."

"No," I said. "You don't *want* to believe in me."

"I believe in myself." He thumped the wrought-iron patio table with his fist. "I believe in this." He nodded toward the town. "And I believe in them, I believe in the war—"

"You are what you eat," I cut in. "Jeff—you *are* what you *eat*!"

He looked stunned. He said nothing.

"You *are* what you *eat*," I said again. "And *I* am what *you* eat, isn't that right, my friend?"

He screamed. He jumped up from the table and ran off into the night.

35

It's going to rain today, I can feel it. The low and ragged line of clouds has come in and the air is moving fitfully, as if it is at war with itself.

These children like the rain. They pretend that they can splash about in the puddles, so they say they want it to rain because, I think, they are children, and they need to pretend.

To the north, halfway to the town, in a field that is overgrown with ragweed and crabgrass, I have seen a woman looking in their direction. I believe that she is probably attractive. I'm not sure. Her features are very even and her eyes are large. She's dressed in something long and white, and she has a gentle, welcoming smile on her lips.

She sings, too, although I can hear no words, only a kind of high humming sound that's not at all unpleasant. I've heard it before, once or twice, here, from the storage area of the house.

Occasionally, the woman looks over at me. And when she does, her smile broadens, her eyes close momentarily, she nods very slightly, and I know that she's telling me something. But I'm not sure what.

I can't move from here, of course, to follow her. Much as I want to. I'm like a lumpy gray rock that has been put in this patio chair as a joke, and I want to call out to her, "I can't move, go away! Take these children with you and go away!" If I could speak that's precisely what I'd tell her.

Morning is not far off. A minute, five minutes, an hour. What do I know about mornings? I've been running from them for eighty years.

Here, I have apologies for everyone. I have apologies for Lemuel and for my father. I have apologies for little red-haired Orry, and especially for poor Georgie, whose head went sploosh into a rock. These are heartfelt apologies, very sincere. The termite begs forgiveness for the house that has fallen into dust around it.

But I wasn't responsible for that, was I? The world had a party and I wasn't invited.

The pond I fished at ninety years ago, with the fishing pole my father gave me for my tenth birthday—a hundred feet of good, strong, and expensive line attached to it—was called Turtle Pond. I have been to many places since my death and I think there are probably a thousand ponds called "Turtle Pond" throughout this country, and ten thousand ten-year-olds fishing in them, hauling in a million trout. It is one of the things the living do. They fish and get wet and they want to grow up.

273

The dead also do most of the things that the living do, except that they do them over and over and over again.

Until they are able to listen. These children do not want to listen. They want to pretend, they want to be children because they're certain that they can be children forever.

From the town I can hear gunfire again, and I know enough about guns to know that there's a little battle going on, that several different kinds of gun are being used—shotguns and rifles and handguns—and that people are dying. Because every once in a while the woman standing in the ragweed and crabgrass takes her gaze off the children and off me and looks in the direction of the town. Then she looks back and I see something in her eyes that is very much like satisfaction, as if she is alone and knows that she will soon have company.

I need this woman.

I don't believe that I am the last vampire. I believe that I'm a human being who was seduced into death eighty years ago.

I believe that I am food for the living.

At last these children have stopped pretending and one by one have drifted off, into the field where the woman is waiting for them. They went reluctantly, of course, being children, as if they were being called in to dinner. They scowled and they said, "No!" in the fitful and insistent way that children have always said no. But at last they went, whispering to themselves that they were tired, anyway, and just a little bored— "Boring!" said a bright-looking blonde girl of seven or eight.

And one of them, a boy with a lot of dark hair, a round face, and many freckles, turned halfway, looked in my direction, smiled, and waved for me to come along, as if to say, "It's okay, you can play too."

And maybe I can.

Morning.
It's cream-colored.
Like milk.

Sips of Blood

MARY ANN MITCHELL

The Marquis de Sade. The very name conjures images of decadence, torture, and dark desires. But even the worst rumors of his evil deeds are mere shades of the truth, for the world doesn't know what the Marquis became—they don't suspect he is one of the undead. And that he lives among us still. His tastes remain the same, only more pronounced. And his desire for blood has become a hunger. Let Mary Ann Mitchell take you into the Marquis's dark world of bondage and sadism, a world where pain and pleasure become one, where domination can lead to damnation. And where enslavement can be forever.

Quenched

MARY ANN MITCHELL

An evil stalks the clubs and seedy hotels of San Francisco's shadowy underworld. It preys on the unfortunate, the outcasts, the misfits. It is an evil born of the eternal bloodlust of one of the undead, the infamous nobleman known to the ages as . . . the Marquis de Sade. He and his unholy offspring feed upon those who won't be missed, giving full vent to their dark desires and a thirst for blood that can never be sated. Yet while the Marquis amuses himself with the lives of his victims, with their pain and their torture, other vampires—of Sade's own creation—are struggling to adapt to their new lives of eternal night. And as the Marquis will soon learn, hatred and vengeance can be eternal as well—and can lead to terrors even the undead can barely imagine.

___4717-9 $5.50 US/$6.50 CAN

VOICE OF THE BLOOD

JEMIAH JEFFERSON

Ariane is desperate for some change, some excitement to shake things up. She has no idea she is only one step away from a whole new world–a world of darkness and decay, of eternal life and eternal death. But once she falls prey to Ricari she will learn more about this world than she ever dreamt possible. More than anyone should dare to know . . . if they value their soul. For Ricari's is the world of the undead, the vampire, a world far beyond the myths and legends that the living think they know. From the clubs of San Francisco to a deserted Hollywood hotel known as Rotting Hxall, the denizens of this land of darkness hold sway over the night. Bur a seductive and erotic as these predators may be, Ariane will soon discover that a little knowledge can be a very dangerous thing indeed.

___4830-2 $5.99 US/$6.99 CAN

Dorchester Publishing Co., Inc.
P.O. Box 6640
Wayne, PA 19087-8640

THE TRAVELING VAMPIRE SHOW
RICHARD LAYMON

It's a hot August morning in 1963. All over the rural town of Grandville, tacked to the power poles and trees, taped to store windows, flyers have appeared announcing the one-night-only performance of The Traveling Vampire Show. The promised highlight of the show is the gorgeous Valeria, the only living vampire in captivity.

For three local teenagers, two boys and a girl, this is a show they can't miss. Even though the flyers say no one under eighteen will be admitted, they're determined to find a way. What follows is a story of friendship and courage, temptation and terror, when three friends go where they shouldn't go, and find much more than they ever expected.

__4850-7 $5.99 US/$6.99 CAN

B|TE RICHARD LAYMON

"No one writes like Laymon, and you're going to have a good time with anything he writes."
—**Dean Koontz**

It's almost midnight. Cat's on the bed, facedown and naked. She's Sam's former girlfriend, the only woman he's ever loved. Sam's in the closet, with a hammer in one hand and a wooden stake in the other. Together they wait as the clock ticks down because . . . the vampire is coming. When Cat first appears at Sam's door he can't believe his eyes. He hasn't seen her in ten years, but he's never forgotten her. Not for a second. But before this night is through, Sam will enter a nightmare of blood and fear that he'll never be able to forget—no matter how hard he tries.

"Laymon is one of the best writers in the genre today."
—**Cemetery Dance**

IN THE DARK

RICHARD LAYMON

Nothing much happens to Jane Kerry, a young librarian. Then one day Jane finds an envelope containing a fifty-dollar bill and a note instructing her to "Look homeward, angel." Jane pulls a copy of the Thomas Wolfe novel of that title off the shelf and finds a second envelope. This one contains a hundred-dollar bill and another clue. Both are signed, "MOG (Master of Games)." But this is no ordinary game. As it goes on, it requires more and more of Jane's ingenuity, and pushes her into actions that she knows are crazy, immoral or criminal—and it becomes continually more dangerous. More than once, Jane must fight for her life, and she soon learns that MOG won't let her quit this game. She'll have to play to the bitter end.

___4916-3 $5.99 US/$6.99 CAN

SPIRIT
GRAHAM
MASTERTON

Peggy Buchanan is such an adorable little girl, all blond curls and sweetness. Then comes the tragic day when her family finds Peggy floating in the icy water of their swimming pool, dead, her white dress billowing around her. Her sisters, Laura and Elizabeth, can't imagine life without Peggy. They know from that day forward their lives will be changed forever. But they can't know the nightmare that waits for them. Peggy may be dead—but she hasn't left them. As the sisters grow up, a string of inexplicable deaths threatens to shatter their lives. No matter how warm the weather, each corpse shows signs of severe frostbite . . . and each victim's dying moments are tortured by a merciless little girl in a white dress, whose icy kiss is colder than death.

___4935-X $5.99 US/$6.99 CAN

PREY

GRAHAM MASTERTON

There's something in the attic of Fortyfoot House. Something that rustles. Something that scampers and scratches. Something with fur. But it isn't a rat. It's something far, far more terrifying than a rat.

Recently divorced, David Williams takes a job restoring Fortyfoot House, a dilapidated nineteenth-century orphanage, hoping to find peace of mind and get to know his young son, Danny. But then he hears the scratching noises in the attic. And he sees long-dead people walking across the lawn.

Does Fortyfoot House exist in today, yesterday, tomorrow—or all three at once? Only one thing is certain—it is a house with a dark, unthinkable secret that threatens to send David's world hurtling into a living nightmare. A nightmare that only David himself can prevent—if he can escape the thing in the attic.

___4633-4 $4.99 US/$5.99 CAN

THE HOUSE THAT JACK BUILT

GRAHAM MASTERTON

Valhalla was built by legendary gambler and womanizer Jack Belias, and every inhabitant since him has met with tragedy. Even today, the mansion echoes with a terrible, agonized sobbing.

When Craig stumbles upon Valhalla he feels a fascination he has never known. He knows it will be the perfect place to save his troubled marriage. His wife, Effie, tries to ignore the horrible feeling the house gives her. But she still hires a spiritualist to rid Valhalla of its fearsome vibrations.

As Craig's obsession with the house grows, he becomes more of a stranger to Effie every day. Could it be that the spirit of the past is still with them?